More

Three Erotic Stories

Candace Wright

Published by: CRBarton Productions, LLC
www.crbarton.com

WARNING: ADULT READING MATERIAL

This story contains scenes of an explicit, erotic nature and is intended for adults, 18+. Characters portrayed are 18 and older.

ISBN: 099787791X
ISBN-13: 978-0997877915

At Her Boss's Command

1 - At Her Boss's Command

Neela woke suddenly in a sweat with her thin, white, silk night shirt soaked all the way through. In her sleep, even the cool air blowing through the air conditioning vents couldn't cool her overheated body when the dream once again invaded her mind and teased her body. She'd been having the same hot, sexy dream about being taken and pleasured in every sexual position possible by several men in her office. She struggled between wanting to get a full night's sleep knowing she had to work the next morning and begging for the dream to become a reality as the men gave her more and more until she begged them to stop, which she knew she never would.

Throwing back the bed covers and climbing out of bed, she went in search of a dry shirt. As she flipped through the dresser for one, the thought

1

crossed her mind that perhaps she should forgo sweating through another shirt and go back to bed without one. It was the reason why, weeks ago, she decided to stop wearing panties to bed. After several mornings of waking up with signs of a dream-filled orgasm between her legs, she knew it was a waste to keep putting them on.

Neela wondered how other women dealt with salacious dreams that gave them just as much satisfaction as the real thing. Did it become a distraction for them as much as it was creating for her? She wanted more than what she told friends she indulged in. She kept it simple with them, thinking the names people would call her behind her back wouldn't be flattering if they knew her proclivity for wild sex and getting the kind of pleasure everyone should be open to giving and receiving. At twenty-six, she'd had enough of what some people would call normal or average sex. She wanted to live on the edge sexually and explore orgasms on another level.

An average woman she wasn't because though she enjoyed sex with a man, she couldn't see herself in a marriage with kids, a house and a pet or two. She wanted mind-blowing orgasms day after day with each getting more experimental and steamier than the one before. The part she tends to leave out of conversations with friends is that she loved to experiment sexually, but not with the same man all the time. Variety was her flavor of choice and she wasn't ashamed at all, at least not in private. She loved variety that came with different size cocks, various talented tongues and positions that weren't found in any book. The norm of one man, one woman was lost on her since she preferred sex a little less tamed.

Recently as her dreams began controlling her night, she no longer cared what anyone thought. Her life, especially the sexual part of it, was all about her and what her needs were, getting them met while holding nothing back. Her dreams were a sign that she wanted and needed more, but how to get it was another story.

Climbing back into bed, this time completely naked, she prepared herself for what was to come. She would fall asleep and find herself in the best possible position with men filling her holes and taking her higher and higher like she craved.

Looking over at the clock blaring red in her darkened bedroom, she had a feeling she was going to have a hard day at work trying to stay focused after getting up several times throughout the night.

Her bosses at her job as a legal secretary in one of the biggest law firms in downtown Dallas didn't appreciate lateness or laziness, which meant a full night's sleep was important. The only thing that worked when there was no man in her bed to give her the relief she needed was one of the many sex toys she kept hidden in various parts of her bedroom. There was a time in her life when she would never consider buying one, but hearing women talk about them all the time made her curious. They did the trick especially when she learned what her body wanted and there were times she knew better how to get it by pleasuring herself than she did from any man.

Sampling a man or two wasn't lost on her and for the past year, Neela found herself unable to resist spreading eagle for them. All she had to do was imaging a big, long, hard cock and her body was ready for the orgasm she knew could follow. She wondered if she were turning into some sort of nymphomaniac. She tried to be conservative about her need for more, but each time she gave herself over to one man, it never seemed to be enough. She always longed for more.

More was what she needed at the moment and her choices were to either make a desperate phone call in the middle of the night to one of her male friends for a booty call or she could get quick relief that was waiting for her in a drawer. She opted for the second option and reached across the bed for her dark chocolate. Oh, how she loved black men and thought that their large, dark penises were a masterful work of art. She loved how they looked against her pearly white, pale skin. The contrast was a major turn-on. That was a secret she told very few of her friends.

Neela came from powerful white money and etiquette was everything to her family and close friends, so chasing behind black cock was not something she would advertise, though secretly, she craved it day in and day out. She didn't care about race and she was ashamed at those closest to her who did. Still her private life was hers and so was her choice of fuck buddies.

Feeling around in the dark, she opened her nightstand and pulled out her trusty nine-inch wonder and reached around for a bottle of lube she knew was in there along with a condom.

Laying back on the bed she opened the condom packet and slowly pulled it down the length of the silicone cock. She didn't really have a need for the lube because she already knew the hot dream had her wetter than the nearest lake. Opening her legs wide, she squirted a little on her fingers anyway and spread it all around her pussy lips making them even wetter so that the nine-inches would slide in easily.

Neela's anxiety to feel the thickness inside of her had her heart rate speeding up and in the quiet of the room, she could hear how hard she was breathing, knowing relief was on the way. Her legs began to quiver as she thought of what the first feel of the cock sliding inside of her would be. There was no need to deny herself any longer as she leaned back until she was comfortable on one of the many pillows that were splayed out across the head of her bed. Already naked, she spread her legs wider and placed the head of the plastic cock on the tip of her clit knowing the action would bring about an exhilarating feeling. Her nub was sensitive at the first touch as her hips lifted slightly from the bed.

Neela knew what was next when she rubbed the cock across her swollen clit sliding it up then down, left then right. With her free hand she reached up and lightly squeezed the tight bud of her nipple before giving the pebbled tip a harder pinch. The glorious feeling was exactly what she needed. She cupped the globe of her breast, first one side and then the other and when she went to pinch the other nipple, she slid the head of the cock inside of her waiting pussy and opened her mouth on a sigh at the thick, hard entry.

"Oh, this feels so good," she said out loud.

It didn't take long to bring herself the gratification she needed. She pulled the length out and slowly slid it back in repeating the movement over and over again, adding in the grind of her hips and the perfect angle so that with each pass into her body, the toy rubbed against her swollen clit. As the feeling of reaching her peak crept up on her, uncontrollably her head flopped from side to side wanting more and more. The spiky feeling began in her feet and traveled up her legs to her pussy. Her body was overstimulated from the feeling of the cock inside of her to the intense feeling as she pinched and pulled on her tits until her hips pistoned up as her hand moved the cock in and out of her faster and faster. She chased that orgasm like never before and just before the magnitude of the wave came over her, an image of two of the attorneys in her office entered her mind with visions of them stripping her naked and filling two of her holes at the same time, the way she knew she would beg them to.

The image of two men taking her sent her over the edge as she screamed through her pleasure, never letting up on the strokes in and out of her body.

As her body calmed from the intense orgasm, she removed the toy and used it to stroke her clit until her body relaxed back on the bed. Another night of self pleasure was fine, but it was nothing compared to having a man in her bed. She didn't want just any man. She wanted one who wasn't about the vanilla type of sex men thought women wanted. She wanted men who gave it to her hard and nasty, holding nothing back. She wished she was bold enough to tell men what she wanted instead of living out her fantasy in her head and sometimes on the internet.

She knew it was time for a change and that change would involve more of what she wanted and needed to be sexually satisfied.

2 - At Her Boss's Command

"Ms. Mason, can you step into my office for a minute please?"

Neela looked up as her boss, Dustin Boone, breezed by her, going straight into his office without looking her way. She grabbed her pen and notepad and leaped from her seat. She tugged at her short skirt trying her best to pull it down below her knees to no avail. She needed to shop for some more suitable office attire. No one said she dressed too sexy, but she knew she did. This was a new Neela, one she sometimes didn't recognize herself. Whether this new Neela was appropriate for the workplace remained to be seen.

There was a time when she never wore her skirts short and tight or her heels higher than two inches. Now she wore five inch heels everyday because she loved how sexy she felt in them and how much longer they made her legs look. She also loved how sexy they made her ass look. Everyone she knew told her she had sexy legs and she decided it was time to show them off more.

She hurried behind Dustin as he entered his office and sat behind his desk. She sat across from him ready to write down notes from the discussion. She was a little distracted as she tended to be whenever she was in his presence.

Neela had been his secretary for six months now and with each passing day, he seemed to get sexier and sexier. The better looking he got, the sexier she seemed to dress, hoping he would notice. He and his two brothers were the owners and partners in the prestigious law firm and one was just as good looking as the other.

The Boone brothers were all over six feet tall, smooth dark chocolate skin, muscles that made her want to stick her tongue out and get a lick and strong strides in their walk that let you know there was some strong power happening between their legs. She longed to find out just how powerful that third leg was. Neela knew she shouldn't have thoughts about her boss in such a sexual way, but she couldn't help herself. Her pussy throbbed the minute he walked by her desk every morning as he entered the office.

"There are some files I need you to pull for me so that I can use them as background for a new case I'm working on," Dustin said.

Neela reached for the list he handed to her across his desk. The glitter of his platinum wedding band glowed bright in her eyes. She had seen pictures of his wife and was jealous knowing the woman was probably getting the best sex of her life every night. She wondered how tempted a man like Dustin Boone could be if the right woman came along offering no commitment, friends with hot sexual benefits sex. She'd like to offer it to him again and again, but she knew it wouldn't happen. He seemed to be dedicated to his wife and was all about business around her. Not once had he given her a sign that he was looking at her in any way other than as his secretary.

The other Boone brothers were pretty much the same. Mark and Malcolm were both single and just as hot. She'd often imagined what it would be like to have all three brothers pleasuring her, which was her ultimate fantasy. Three men at once would be as close to the perfect situation for her as she could get, but she didn't know how a woman went about doing such a thing without compromising her public persona. Clearly word about a woman who loved taking on three men would get out, especially around the office. She would have to quit her job and find another one if she indulged and anyone found out. That was the risky part of coming out of her sexual shell.

Turning her attention back to the meeting, she looked over the list and would go directly to the records room as soon as they were finished. There were paper files of all of the firm's cases and in those files, they also kept a portable disk with the same information for staff who preferred electronic records over paper.

"Yes sir," she replied.

She met Dustin's eyes as he looked up at her.

"Neela, you don't have to call me sir. I told you when you first started that you should feel comfortable calling me Dustin when we're alone. You only need to address me as Mr. Boone when clients are around and never call me sir."

Neela smiled. She'd forgotten again.

"I'm sorry. I keep forgetting you told me that. I was accustomed to saying sir on my last job and it's a hard habit to break."

"Not a problem. Why don't you go ahead and get those files so that I can start reviewing them. Email the electronic files to me and I'll finish reviewing them when I get home tonight."

"Will there be anything else?" she asked. Perhaps a nice, sloppy blow job, she said to herself. The man was just so damn fine.

"Nothing else for now. I'm leaving early today so feel free to make it an early day for yourself. The next few nights I'm going to need you to stay late to help me prepare for this case and we'll probably be here pretty late, so take advantage of the extra time off today. Try to make whatever arrangements you need to make to stay until at least midnight for the next four or five nights."

"That's not a problem. I didn't have anything planned."

She watched at Dustin leaned back in his big leather office chair and focused his attention on her as if he was shocked to hear that she didn't have anything to do once she left work.

"You don't have a boyfriend or anyone else who would be angry with you spending that many days and nights here in the office?"

Neela blushed. She and Dustin didn't have many personal chats because the office was always busy with work. She was surprised he actually asked her something that wasn't business related.

"Nope, no boyfriend at the moment. I do hang out with friends on the weekend, but I wasn't planning to do that this weekend, so I'm all yours," she said, using words that had a double meaning for her.

"I like the sound of that," he said in a tone that to her, sounded seductive. That couldn't be right, she thought.

She matched his gaze and looked over at him and she couldn't mistake the hint of something in the way he was looking at her. He had the deepest, darkest eyes she'd ever seen and every time he looked at her, he drew her in and he didn't even know it. He made a woman want to cream just by the way he looked at her. Usually everything about him was business around her, but his last comment was laced with something else and she liked it. Thankful for the little vibrator in her purse, she needed to find a secret place quick. She needed relief. She stood to leave before she did something like dropped to her knees, begged him to let her take out his cock so that he could gag her with it.

"I'm going to get right on those files and I'll be at my desk if you need anything."

"You look very nice today Neela."

Uh oh, she thought. A compliment on her attire combined with his deep voice was almost too much to handle. She wondered if there were days that he felt she dressed too sexy, but since she'd upped her game, she received more and more compliments from him. She liked the new her and she knew that people sometimes claimed that white women didn't have big asses, but she was the exception and the tight, form fitting skirts she wore showed off her slim waist that led down to her apple bottom.

"Thank you," she said shyly. She hoped as she left, he would take a look at her ass in her tight skirt. When she dressed in the morning, she did so with him in mind.

Before heading to the records room, Neela grabbed her purse and went to the private bathroom to hit herself off real quick so that she could focus on work and not on how badly she needed a big cock in her.

Reaching the bathroom, she made quick work of pulling out the small vibrator in her purse. She was so anxious to come that her fingers were shaking. After making sure no one was in any of the other stalls, she went in the one furthest from the door and locked it once she was inside. Sliding her black laced panties down her legs and leaning against the wall of the bathroom stall, she slid her skirt up over her hips and as she closed her eyes. Her first act was to slip a finger inside of her pussy, not surprised when a flood of moisture coated her fingers. That was the impact every encounter with Dustin Boone had on her. She turned the vibrator on low so that it hummed very light and stroked her clit with it until it grew hard under her ministrations. Maneuvering herself for the best possible position in the stall, she used her other hand to insert two fingers in her pussy and rode them while running the vibrator across her clit. With visions of Dustin in her head naked and pumping into her body from behind, before long, she held her lips tight as a powerful orgasm ripped through her to the point where she almost collapsed to the floor.

The door to the bathroom opened as someone entered and she quickly gathered herself and put her friendly toy away in her purse. She fixed her clothes, flushed the toilet she never used and then exited the stall. She smiled at one of the other secretaries as she washed her hands and headed back to her desk hoping to focus better now that she'd taken care of her pesky libido.

Walking out, she headed straight for the records room to get the files Dustin needed. Like most days, she was a woman in heat every time she encountered her boss. Looking at him made her panties wet and whenever they had a meeting, she would leave it on the brink of an orgasm. She knew if she even touched herself, she would explode and so she began packing a vibrator. Neela smiled as she wondered what the security guards thought about her when she had to put her purse on the conveyor belt to be scanned each morning. They had to get a glimpse of it. Perhaps it was why they gave her an extra smile and wave when she entered. Men loved a sexually free woman, especially one who carried a vibrator in her purse to work.

Grabbing what she needed, she headed back to her desk and fought the need to take another trip to the bathroom every time Dustin or one of his brothers walked by.

3- At Her Boss's Command

Leaving the office early gave Neela too much free time. She didn't feel like going anywhere and like most days, she couldn't get beyond the fact that she was horny again. She seemed to be in that state most days. She wasn't in the mood for inviting anyone over so she did what she liked doing when she had the time; to the internet she went. There were always a ton of men on-line who liked to get off and she loved helping them do it while seeking out her own pleasure through the fantasies she lived out in the conversations she had with them.

After getting a quick shower, she slipped on a white thong with matching bra and her black strappy high heels. Grabbing her laptop, she lay across her bed and logged on.

The men were hot tonight, she thought as the pinging sound of a new message went off time after time in rapid succession. She responded to the first on the list, a familiar online friend.

"Hi there Tom," she typed.

"Lily, it's nice to see you on-line again. I'm been looking for you every day," he responded.

She never used her real name making sure to keep her identity a secret. Luckily the site gave free memberships to women while the men had to pay.

"I thought about you and decided to log on and see if you were around," she lied. Whatever floated his boat, she thought.

"I've been thinking about you too since the last time. You were so hot. I hope I'll get to see that ass tonight. Are you turning on your camera?"

"I will in a little bit. Have you been a bad boy Tom?" she typed.

"Oh yes," he answered quickly. "I've been really bad. I know you've been a naughty girl who could probably use a really hard spanking. Let's turn on our microphones," he suggested.

"Sure."

Neela cut on her microphone.

"Is this better?" she spoke saucily.

"Yes baby. So tell me, what are you wearing tonight?"

"I have on a white thong, bra and of course heels, just like you like."

"Damn, I want you more and more every time I talk to you."

"Would you like to see?"

"Yes, yes!" Tom proclaimed anxiously.

"Turn on your camera first so that I can see how much you want me," she said seductively.

Neela waited a few seconds until a vision of Tom from the waist down appeared on her screen.

"There's my big boy," she said seeing his hard cock almost poking into the computer screen. She loved playing online with him. He loved lots of dirty talk and he loved being on camera for her. She clicked the button and turned on her camera making sure to not show her face. She loved to play, but loved her privacy.

"I love you Lily," Tom exclaimed as he began stroking his hard cock for her.

"That's it. Show Lily how much you want to fuck her. I've been horny all day and I need a nice fat cock like yours to satisfy me."

Neela slid the camera further down so that Tom could see her pussy as she opened her legs wide and moved the thong to the side.

"Oh, look at that sweet pussy. I want to lick it for you," he said, stroking even harder and faster.

Neela had a feeling this little interlude wouldn't last long or at least Tom wouldn't. She liked him, but he had a penchant for coming quicker than she wanted him to and she had to find another guy online so that she could get off. Tom was one of her favorites because like some, he had a very big cock and his imagination ran wild.

"Mmm, it's all for you Tom. You look like you're ready to burst," she said as she listened to his breathing get louder and louder through the speakers.

"I am and only you can make me come this fast. Here it comes," he screamed.

Neela watched as Tom barely remained in his seat while his orgasm tore his body apart. Just as she was about to rub one out along with him, her cell phone chimed. She grabbed it and saw a message from one of her many male friends.

'Hey sexy. I was thinking about stopping by real quick to see you.'

Normally she didn't appreciate quick drive-bys, but his timing was perfect.

'You got something for me?'

She knew he knew what she meant.

'Of course. Are you ready for it?'

'I'm right here waiting,' she replied.

'I'm downstairs.'

'Come.'

That was all she needed to type. She closed her laptop without acknowledging Tom, placed it on the floor under her bed and went to the door. As soon as she heard Terrance's knock, she opened it.

"Were you just in the neighborhood?" she asked wiggling her round ass in her thong at him.

"Shit, it's a good thing if I was. Look at you. You are one fine ass woman."

"Well, come in and show me how fine you think I am."

Neela moved to the side as Terrance entered and

they got right down to things as usual.

Moving to the wall beside the door, she planted her hands high on it while spreading her legs. She looked back over her shoulder at Terrance who was already unzipping his pants and pulling out a condom. They didn't need a lot of idle chatter since he was there for one reason.

"Fuck me," she said like a cat purring.

Terrance didn't respond. He moved between her legs, slid her thong to the side and holding on tightly to her hips, he found the entrance to her sopping wet pussy and pushed in, causing them both to exhale with delight.

"I fucking love this pussy of yours," he said with a pump on each word.

"You always show up at the precise moment when this kitty-cat needs you," Neela said panting with excitement.

"I know what you need baby and Terrance is always ready to provide it to you. You like this?"

Neela loved it as she closed her eyes and enjoyed the feel of his cock fucking her good, hard and deep.

"I need it harder baby," she moaned. She loved cock and Terrance had one that could make a woman with no tone, sing a happy tune. Pushing back into his hard thrusts, her mind drifted to Dustin as a vision of him behind his desk stroking his hard cock came to mind. In the vision, he stood slowly, walked over to her and pushed her face into his desk. Next, he spread her legs, hiked up her skirt and pushed his hard cock into her over and over again while telling her that he'd been dreaming about fucking her since she started working for him. The thought of him doing nasty things to her had her body spiraling out of control. Terrance was fucking her, but in her mind, it was Dustin and she went wild.

Terrance increased his strokes, going in deeper and deeper.

Neela felt the rise of an orgasm and Terrance, knowing her body, reached around to tease her clit and the moment she needed came with a flash of light behind her eyes. She held her lips tight as she came over and over, afraid if she said anything, she would scream out Dustin's name. Just as she was coming down, she heard Terrance grunt as his release flooded from him in wave after wave of heated delight.

They stood like that against the wall until Terrance finally pulled out of her body. Her legs were so shaky, she thought any minute that she would collapse to the floor.

"You are always ready for me. I like that."

"You mean, Carly isn't ready for you like this when you get home?" she asked sheepishly.

She often teased him about the fact that he had a girlfriend at home, yet he came to her for sex. She had no qualms about it, but she loved picking with him about it.

Terrance walked into the bathroom and a few

seconds later, came out zipping his pants back up.

"You know how she is and if you'd tell me you're ready to be mine, I'd leave her in a minute and make you my girl. You're playing around and won't give a brother a chance though. I know you love cock and I can give you all the cock you been getting from me and other guys. I can handle your sex drive and you know it. What's up with us being a couple?"

Neela slid her saturated thong down her legs.

"Terrance, you know how I feel about that. I'm good with how things are for me and I like you, you know that. Let's not get all into feelings and tell me if I'll see you this weekend," she crooned and gave him pouty lips that she knew he loved. He could never deny her anything when she played coy.

"Okay, no more pestering you about us and if you want to see me this weekend, I'll be here. You know I can never get enough of you," Terrance said leaning down to kiss her lips.

"Where does Carly think you are?"

"She thinks I'm on my way to my mother's house, which I am, but not before coming by here to get some of this delicious pussy first. You are sexy and love to fuck which is the perfect combination. I may stop back by later tonight if you're game and maybe then we can make it to the bed."

"I'll be here and as always, this pussy will be ready."

Terrance kissed her again and left. Locking the

door, she went to the bathroom to shower and get ready for bed. She looked forward to getting hit off later if he came back, but more importantly, she was looking forward to seeing Dustin in the morning. They were about to begin the first of a few days of working well into the evening. This would be her first time working late with him. Usually he chose others from the staff to help him prepare for a case and they'd get together in the conference room to plan out his strategy. She'd know because the next morning, it would be her job to put all of the files they left out on the table away. She was now going to be joining the team and wanted to do a good job. She had to remember to take her trusty vibrator with her just in case temptation got the best of her. Tomorrow was going to be a good day, she thought as she stepped into the shower.

4- At Her Boss's Command

Neela yawned for the third time. She and Dustin had been working late for the past three nights preparing for his big case. She was surprised to find that this time, he didn't pull together a team of assistants and paralegals to help him; it was just him and her. Each night he ordered food for them and the office desk and floor was littered with papers and files. She knew that he met with other teams in the conference room, but he told her that since it was just the two of them, they could use the large table in his office to work at.

It was almost ten at night and they had been working non-stop since the office closed at six. After Dustin also yawned for the third time, she suggested he get home to get some sleep.

"I know it seems like I'm sleepy, but I'm not. This case is exhausting and my eyes are tired from reading all of these briefs. Let's take a break from work and relax before diving back in."

Neela watched as he dropped the papers he was reading and leaned back in his chair to stretch his long legs out. She stood from the hardback chair, walked over to the leather sofa and sat down. She needed to give her ass and back a break from sitting up straight for four hours. Dustin stood and walked over to his desk and took out a bottle of wine.

"Would you like a glass?" he asked.

"I probably shouldn't. A glass of wine is like potato chips, you can't have just one."

"You can have as many as you like and if you're worried about driving, I can have my driver take you home and you can take the train to work tomorrow to pick it up or I can have someone bring it to you in the morning. You don't relax enough. Have a glass," he said, hitting her with his one hundred watt smile.

Whew, goodness, she thought.

He was right that she needed to relax more and a glass of wine would be perfect.

"Okay, I'd love one."

She stood and took the filled glass from him and sat back down as she watched him take several gulps of his. They sat in silence for a few minutes. Neela didn't know what to say if their conversation wasn't about work.

"So why is it that you don't have a boyfriend?" he asked.

Neela looked over at him and wondered why he decided to leap into that conversation. She knew it probably stemmed from the other day when he asked her if anyone would gripe about her staying late at work. .

"I don't know. I like to date, but nothing too serious and not just with one man," she said sipping the delicious dark wine. It felt smooth going down he throat.

She saw Dustin's eyebrows rise as if he didn't just hear her say she gave her pussy up to more than one man at a time. She didn't actually say that, but if he thought it, he wouldn't be wrong. He was a lawyer, so he knew how to read between the lines.

"You know years ago women who dated several men at a time would be shunned and cast out. There was a negative connotation where as it was okay for a man to do that. In fact, men were praised for keeping up with all of his women," Dustin explained.

"Well, times have changed and I'm a believer that what's good for a man is just as good for a woman," she said and meant it.

"That's true. I believe the same thing."

"I'm sure if I had a boyfriend or a husband, he may not be so understanding of these late hours. How does your wife handle all of your late nights? Does she ever get jealous or wonder if you're actually working?"

"She wonders all of the time, but we have a very

open marriage. Jealousy is never an issue in my marriage."

"Open marriage? So does that mean you both get to see other people on the side outside of your marriage and it's okay?"

"Sort of. I get to do that, she doesn't."

Neela looked at him and frowned.

"What?" she asked.

"Before you chop my head off, I'm not saying she can't; she chooses not to. Anytime she wants to, I'm okay with it, but trust me when I tell you, I give it to her right every single time and she's too exhausted to think of being with another man."

"Does that mean she's not enough for you?"

To her, the conversation was getting good.

"She's plenty, but there's always room for more and a lot of women aren't being satisfied at home or in general and I love lending a helping hand or other body parts," Dustin snickered.

"That's one of the reasons why I don't do relationships. I like the variety that comes with dating several men and they all know there is nothing serious about hanging out with me and we get what we come for."

She watched as Dustin took in her words, trying to decipher how far he could go with this conversation. If he could, then she could too. He had no idea how much she's wanted him and if she had the chance now that she knew he wasn't a one woman man, she would be all over it.

"Do you date outside of your race? Any black men?"

"Race is not an issue for me and I have a fetish for black men."

Dustin's stare was as erotic as they come. The way he was looking at her made her feel like the main feast at a holiday mean.

"What is an issue for you?" he asked.

Neela didn't know how much to share. Though they were relaxed and sharing, he was still her boss.

"It depends on how personal we're talking. I like men who are fun to be around."

"That's it? Just fun?"

"Well, since you and your wife have this open marriage, do you just do it for the fun? Is it that she doesn't care or is it that she doesn't know who, that makes that work out for you. Do you actually date or is it something else?"

"You want honesty?" he asked.

"Yes, of course. We're being all honest and everything right?" she quipped.

Dustin smiled back at her and drummed his fingers on his desk, really getting into their chat.

"Yes, we are. Well, I don't actually date. I do have a wife for dating purposes. This open marriage thing could be better explained by saying I'm just out to fuck other women. No pretense, no promises, just good old fucking."

Hearing him say that woke her right up. Any feeling of being tired went out the window. She looked over at him and noticed that he hadn't batted an eye when he said that.

"Well, we are being personal aren't we?" she said smiling.

"Shall we talk about something else like sports perhaps? I don't want to make you uncomfortable, but you did ask and I am a man who speaks my mind. It's the lawyer in me, I guess."

"True and no, I'm not uncomfortable," she admitted. What she really wanted to say was that he was making her hornier than she ever remembered being in her life.

"I know you're not," Dustin added.

Neela heard something different in his voice, something deep and sexual like she heard the other day when he complimented her on her short, tight skirt. She should be embarrassed at the direction of the conversation, but she wasn't. If he wanted to play, she wasn't one to back down from a challenge.

"So, these women you fuck, are they here at the office or do you pick them up at other places?"

Neela's body drummed sexily when she heard the word, fuck, come out of her own mouth, directing it at her boss, the man who starred in many of her erotic dreams.

To show that she wasn't skittish about the conversation, she asked her question, placed her now empty wine glass on the table beside the chair and laid back. She was nothing if she wasn't comfortable.

"Okay, so we're having this conversation then."

Dusting leaned back comfortably.

"Oh, yes, we are," Neela said, making sure her words sounded inviting.

"Well, I have never played here at work or with anyone from work, but that doesn't mean I won't. I don't go looking for women, but I know when I want one when I meet her."

"Is that so? And just what does this woman typically look like?" she asked.

"Well, she looks like the type that's willing to open her legs, shut her mouth and swallow my cock when I tell her to," he said boldly.

Damn! She thought. Her kind of man.

"Lucky women," she replied just as bold.

"It usually turns out that we're both lucky actually. What about you? In all this dating, are some of these guys getting lucky? Do they get to see what's under those tight, short skirts you wear? I bet there are boners everywhere you go."

Neela looked down at herself, happy to know he had been noticing and hoped he was one of the guys with a boner.

"Honestly, most of them do. Why serial date if it's not about the sex. If I wanted anything more than that, I'd be in a relationship and I don't do those right now. For me, it's about the pleasure."

"I see you Neela," Dustin said, leaning back even further in his office chair and removing the tie that he'd loosened earlier.

"I see you too," she said meeting his stare without blinking.

"So, in your opinion, is this conversation inappropriate?" Dustin asked.

"Only for someone other than me," she responded without hesitation.

"Did your skirts get tighter and shorter for me? By the way, nice ass."

"Yes they did and trust me my ass looks even better without the skirt on."

"Oh, I have a feeling that ass of yours is everything. I've had a few boners looking at it."

That's exactly what she wanted to hear. Her excitement was off the charts. It's now or never, she thought.

"Is that boner present now?" she asked with no hint of shyness.

"I'm an alpha male when it comes to women and sex. If that doesn't scare you, why don't you come a little closer and find out for yourself."

Challenge accepted, she thought.

5- At Her Boss's Command

Neela didn't hesitate. This is what her fantasies have been about and this wasn't the time to be squeamish or shy. She got up and walked over to Dustin who turned his office chair around to face her. When she was in view of his crotch, her thoughts of how big his cock would be didn't do him justice. His cock stood big and thick in his pants and she was more than ready to set it free. She licked her lips showing him she was impressed by the imprint of his large cock and large cocks were her obsession.

"Take your top off," he demanded not taking his eyes off of her.

Neela looked down to unbutton her blouse.

"Look up at me and don't take your eyes off of me," he declared.

Her body tingled at the command like never

before. The power behind his voice had her hotter than fire. The moment was more erotic than she'd ever anticipated. The thong she had on was already drenched in her juices and she was still fully clothed. She unbuttoned her blouse and slid it down her arms.

"The rest," he demanded with authority.

She reached behind her back and unzipped her skirt which then fell to the floor in a heap. She reached up to unclasp the front closure of her bra and let it fall to her feet as well. Just as she reached to slide her thong down her legs, he stopped her.

"Leave that on for now. You look sexy in that strip of thong and your heels. I love a sexy ass woman in heels and an ass made for a thong."

Neela watched as he signaled for her to drop to her knees in front of him and as she did, she watched as he unbuckled and then unzipped his pants. When he reached inside and pulled out his cock, her mouth watered in anticipation of getting it in her mouth. He was only semi-hard and she could see he was bigger than any man she'd ever been with. How many nights had she swallowed the plastic lover in her nightstand imagining that it was Dustin? The reality was better than any dream she could ever have. She was more than ready to get a taste of his monster cock.

Her eyes followed his every move as he kept his eyes locked on her while he stroked himself. As he stroked, she watched his face and his eyes told her he couldn't wait for her to take him in her mouth and she was ready to oblige. Her fetish was for big, black cock and Dustin was about to help her satisfy her need for his.

"I have some dictation I'd like for you to take," he said sliding forward in the chair so that he could spread his legs wide enough for her to fit in between them.

He held his cock out for her like a snake charmer to a snake, waving it from side to side. She felt hypnotized as her head followed every move of his cock moving back and forth. She moved with a swiftness licking her lips just before leaning her head down and licking around the fat head of his cock. She moaned when her tongue came in contact with him, hard under her tongue.

"That's it. Go slow with it, savor it and make sure you get it nice and wet," Dustin said.

Neela obliged like she never has before. She opened her mouth a little more as she slid her mouth over the head and down the shaft.

Her excitement rose even more when she heard Dustin moan under her tongue ministrations.

"Take all you can. I want to feel the back of your throat," Dustin proclaimed through gritted teeth.

Neela knew a lot of things about herself and one thing she knew was that she was good at giving head. She had practiced enough on her toys and she'd gotten enough kudos from men who told her she sucked head better than any woman they'd ever known. She wanted to make sure Dustin felt the same way, as she focused on making sure she pleasured him to his liking.

She licked the head and sucked around it before going all the way back down on it again making sure the head hit up against the back of her throat.

Dustin groaned with pleasure and she smiled slightly.

"That's it. Ah, yeah that's good."

Dustin pumped his hips up going further in her mouth while he held her head in between his hands guiding her movements the way he liked.

"I told you this is how I like women and this view is magnificent only matched by the feel of your hot ass mouth. Work this cock, Neela."

She did what she was told and gave everything she had. She was so focused on pleasing his cock that she didn't hear that someone had entered the office.

"So this is what you've been doing for the past few nights of working late."

Neela stopped and looked up to see that Dustin's younger brother Malcolm had entered the office and where she should have been embarrassed, she wasn't. Something in her hoped that he would join them. To show that she wasn't shy with his presence, she leaned her head back down and took Dustin's cock back into her mouth again, this time with her eyes on Malcolm, letting him see how much she loved sucking cock. She wanted him to imagine his sinking deep in her mouth too.

"What's up, bro. No, this is the first night for this, but I'm getting the feeling it won't be the last. I've discovered that Neela here is a little minx who loves cock and I felt it was my duty to find out just how much. As you can see your presence hasn't startled her one bit. I think I feel an extra zest in her sucking skills since you walked in and her mouth is incredible. You should get in on this, isn't that right Neela?" Dustin asked looking down at her.

Neela didn't want to take his cock out of her mouth since she was enjoying it too much, so she nodded her head yes as she slurped him like a lollipop.

"Oh, I see what's happening here. You don't mind if I join in? You are a little minx huh. Willing to take more than one cock?"

Neela moaned loud enough for them both to hear her.

"I think she likes the idea. You know I've never had a problem sharing a woman or two with my brothers. It looks to me like she's looking for double action," Dustin said.

"Nothing better than a woman who really loves cock and doesn't have a problem when more than one joins the party," Malcolm added, walking closer to them while taking his cock out of his pants.

"Why don't you come get some of this. I want a different entry point," Dustin said standing up.

"Stay on your knees," he commanded her and Neela stayed in position.

Neela watched as Malcolm quickly removed his shirt, pants and boxers and stroked himself. He backed up and walked backwards to the sofa and sat down, inviting Neela to join him.

"Stay on your knees," he said.

Getting orders played havoc with her psyche. The power behind their voices gave her a rise like never before. She could feel her juices soaking her thong and slide down the inside of her legs.

Crawling over to him, she eased in between his legs as he pulled her close, gripping the back of her head. Malcolm's cock was just as big as Dustin's so she knew she was in for a real treat. After nudging her mouth open with the head of his cock, she opened even wider and took him in. She licked around it like it was an ice cream cone, making sure he knew that she enjoyed it and wanted more.

While she pleasured him, she heard the sounds of a condom wrapper tearing just before she felt Dustin kneel down behind her. She adjusted position as he raised her hips for easy access. Dustin slid her thong to the side and slowly guided his cock into her pussy, easing in inch by inch. Neela had never felt so full in her life. The feeling of one cock in her mouth and one in her pussy was better than any imagination or dream she'd ever had.

"Damn, you are nice and tight," Dustin said as

he increased his pumps into her pussy from behind. Neela pushed back into him wanting to feel every single glorious inch of him and enjoying the sound throughout the room that magnified the sounds of them fucking. She slurped at Malcolm's cock as her body signaled she was on the verge of a powerful orgasm. She wanted to prolong it, but the feeling was so good she couldn't fight it. When the powerful surge seared through her, she rode out her pleasure taking Malcolm even deeper into her mouth as she arched her back to take even more of Dustin in.

"That's it baby girl," Dustin said.

Neela felt him grip her hips tighter as he pistoned in and out of her, turning her on even more with the sound of his strong thighs slapping against her ass. Giving her even more, he gave her ass a light pat and when she wiggled as her orgasm went on and on, she encouraged him to pat her a little harder and he did causing her to soar again into a second orgasm. She never stopped her sucking motion on Malcolm and when his hips pushed harder toward her face she felt him explode in her mouth. She relaxed her throat to make sure she didn't miss a drop.

Behind her Dustin pushed her ass down a little further and on a guttural, animalist groan, he came and rocked into her so hard her knees lifted off of the floor with each lunge into her pussy.

"Damn, if I had known your pussy was this good,

I would have gotten in this the moment you started working for me. I don't usually play at the office, but this ass is worth it and I needed this."

"Bro, you have one hell of a secretary here and I see she loves taking orders. Let me know the next time the two of you decide to work late," Malcolm said while trying to catch his breath.

Neela wiped her mouth and looked up at him.

"Well, Dustin and I have one more night of working late if you find you have some late night work you have to do also. I'm here to please day and night," she added, making reference to her hard work as his secretary during the day and his sex slave at night. She was hoping this time was not the first and last time with them.

"We're all on the same page, right Neela?" Dustin asked.

"If your page is giving me more of all this good cock, then yes, we're on the same page. This beats my nights of toys at home. I told you I'm serial when it comes to men and I have no expectations other than getting fucked good."

Malcolm smiled, liking the sound of that.

"In that case, I'll be sure to join you tomorrow and perhaps a little one on one time for me too every now and then as long as my brother is good with that," Malcolm said and looked between her and Dustin.

"Hey, Neela is her own woman and I think even adding the two of us to the mix, she still craves more. Isn't that right Neela? It's all about the cock."

"Yes it is and the more the merrier. Perhaps Mark has some late night work he has to get done tomorrow night?" she said looking between them to let them know she was down for whatever.

"Oh, I have no doubt he'll find some after I clue him in. You hit the jackpot hiring this one, Dustin. I need to get out of here and get to my date."

"You're in here fucking around and you have a date waiting?"

"Yup, but this was more important. I'll see you tomorrow in the office and tomorrow night right back here and with Mark in tow. I say let's make use of your office bedroom. I want to get this girl stretched out," Malcolm added.

"That sounds good to me," Neela added, already excited for what the next night will bring with all three brothers. Now that she'd experienced the hotness, she wasn't ready to go back to enjoying her toys in the drawer.

"What happens after our last night of working late here in the office? I guess I'll have to make up excuses for working late more often," Dustin said.

"I have a solution. Whenever we aren't working late, I'm always up late at home and I hope you'll feel free to give me a call anytime. I don't live far from the office," Neela looking from one brother and then to the other. She smiled when both men nodded.

"I like the sound of that," Dustin said and

Malcolm shook his head signaling he was on board too. She was happy to know she'd be getting some new late night visitors.

Still on her knees with Dustin deep inside of her, she felt him rise again and quivered when he wiggled against her ass.

"Looks like the two of you have more work to do, so I'll leave you to it."

"You do that while I take your place on the sofa and since Neela is already on her needs, I want to feel her hot mouth sliding on my cock again. Tonight is still young.

Neela smiled that she finally got to live out her fantasy and was ready for even more.

Dustin got up and sat on the sofa, removing the spent condom and pointing the head of his cock at her mouth. With no hesitation at all, she placed her mouth over his cock, tasting him and got what she wanted and needed. She wanted more and her boss provided it. She knew there would be no more need for hot dreams when she could live it out in real time. That was her last thought before lowering her head and swallowing Dustin's cock again. Dreams do come true, she thought.

What Happens in Vegas

1 – What Happens in Vegas

"Welcome to Las Vegas," the hotel staffer said as Torrie, her sister Natalie and the other members of the bridal party entered, excited about the weekend. This was the first time for most of them in Vegas and Torrie couldn't wait to see if the new resort was all she'd heard and read about.

Her sister Natalie was the reigning bride-to-be and Torrie knew it was her job to make sure she sent her off to her new life as a married woman with one last hoorah! There was no better place than Vegas to do that.

"Thank you very much. I'm Torrie English and we're checking in. The reservation for the suite should be in my name," she said handing over her identification.

"This place is nice," Natalie said looking around.

"Yes, it is. It's the newest hotel on the strip and is less than a year old. I'm told it includes the best amenities over every other spot here and we, my friends, are booked into the penthouse suite that comes with everything you can imagine including a couple of indoor pools and we each get our own suite with a king sized bed and en-suite. You're going to love it," Torrie said.

"I'm so ready for the weekend," Dyanna, one of the bridesmaids chimed in.

In all, there were eight of them on this trip to Vegas and including herself, who was serving as maid of honor, there were six bridesmaids, Dyanna, Kim, Rina, Alyssa, Angel and Paris. In one month, her sister, Natalie, was going to marry the man of her dreams, but before that, Torrie was going to show her the weekend of her life.

She had plans for them to take in a drag queen show, a comedy show, clubbing, the best in dinner, never ending drinks and to start off their weekend, they were going to be entertained in their own suite by the hottest male dancers money could garner. Every woman she asked who she knew had been to Vegas recommended the same company which had the best dancers in Vegas. She was told they employed men of all ages and races and she specifically requested a variety of each.

"I can't begin to tell you how much in need I was for this weekend!" Alyssa added.

All the women nodded in agreement and had

promised to leave their home lives back in Cincinnati where they were from. This weekend was about having the time of their lives and that's exactly what they were going to do.

"Your suite is ready for you," the receptionist said signally for three men to come over.

"Ladies, these men will gather your luggage and escort you to your penthouse suite on the top floor. You have the biggest and best suite in the hotel and I'd like to again personally welcome you to Las Vegas. I know you're going to have a wonderful time and if you need anything at all, there is someone available to assist you around the clock for your entire stay."

All of the ladies shrieked in excitement as they chatted back and forth.

"Do you know if all of my requests for the room were completed? I know we're a little early," she said, whispering so that the others couldn't hear her. She made sure she put all the bells and whistles in place for her sister's special weekend.

"Yes, all of your instructions and requests were followed."

Torrie slipped her a very large tip and followed the group to the elevator.

"What's up first for us this weekend?" Natalie asked as she straightened the sash that crossed her body with the words 'bride' written across it.

"Well, for starters, remember you have to wear a different 'bride' sash every time we leave the hotel.

Tonight is our in-suite party night and the only night you have to wear one inside."

Natalie looked at her sister with a side-eye.

"What craziness do you have planned for tonight? I know it's going to be wild because I know you!" she exclaimed.

Torrie smiled with a devious grin knowing she had an over-the-top night planned and spared no expense when it came to spending Ray's money.

Luckily she was engaged to a thirty million dollar national basketball star center who had no problem splurging on her every want and need and this weekend, she wanted and needed the best of everything. The fifty thousand dollar a night suite was only the beginning.

"Just keep your panties on and wait and see," she said, walking out of the elevator when they reached the top floor.

They walked a few steps when one of the men who brought up their luggage, opened the door to the suite and all of the ladies stood looking around with their mouths hung wide open. The suite was immaculate, exemplifying the life of the rich and famous and there was bling, glitter and expensive décor everywhere.

"Each of you has your own room and there is an outside and indoor pool, both with a Jacuzzi. Each room comes with a king size bed, your own bathroom en-suite, large walk in closets and each leads to the patio that circles the entire building.

The outside pool goes the entire length of one wall of your suite. The bar is fully stocked and you will have your very own wait staff and cooks who will cook tonight's dinner and anything else you want to eat at any time. They can also make any and every drink you can think of. They'll be here by six tonight to begin setting up. The chef will be here at five and we'll have everything he will need delivered based on the menu that's planned for tonight. Your luggage will be placed in your rooms that have already been assigned by Ms. Torrie and if there is anything you find you need, there is a direct line to your personal attendant. That line is staffed around the clock until you check out."

Torrie was as shocked as the other ladies, though she had taken a virtual tour on-line of the suite months ago to make sure it was what she wanted. The biggest enhancement since then was the addition of the decorations that were done to her specifications.

"Oh, this weekend is on!" Torrie exclaimed. She followed everyone as they checked out every room.

"This place even includes it's very own gym, theater room and hair and nail salon. This is crazy cool!" Kim said as they ventured from room to room to see what else it included.

"Amazing!" Natalie said.

"Ms. Torrie, if you need anything at all, don't hesitate to call down. Your every need is our priority."

Torrie reached for a tip and the men stopped her.

"That has already been taken care of very nicely by Mr. Ray."

Ray was the best and the fact that he spared no expense when she asked had her beaming with pride.

"Thank you," she said as they turned and left.

"What the hell should we do first?" Natalie asked.

"Let's shower and change and take in a little of Vegas before tonight."

"Torrie, what's happening tonight and should I be afraid?" Natalie said smiling.

Torrie winked at her.

"You should be very afraid. Just be ready for a fun night. Now let's go see Vegas. This adventure is just beginning."

2 – What Happens in Vegas

The Friday night party in their suite was in full swing. This is the part of the Vegas trip where details would stay in Vegas. The male entertainers had arrived and were currently taking turns performing and each one was hotter than the previous one.

Torrie was pleased with the men she selected for their first night of fun. One of the guys was a surprise and an incredible surprise he was. He substituted for one of the men who had a last minute emergency and she couldn't have asked for a better replacement. They were some of the sexiest she'd ever encountered and when she inquired about men for the evening who were open to pleasing, not only on the dance floor, but in the bedroom as well if any of the women decided they really wanted to let their hair down, she was told what the men decided to do was totally up to them, but that anything was possible. She read between the lines, knowing this was Vegas and foamed at the mouth at the thought that she and not just her sister would be able to get an itch or two scratched. The weekend was an all out, do whatever you want, kind of weekend and each lady was more than ready to indulge.

They were the closest of friends and they would never, ever tell each other's secrets. This weekend was meant to be full of fun and an unwavering lack of inhibitions. Torrie couldn't think of a better way to start it off than with fresh meat and she was looking at eight such men. Each were built and sculpted to perfection with cock imprints that would make a girl salivate on sight. She herself had a secret obsession for the male cock, unlike anything she'd ever tell anyone about. That was her secret and she planned to live out a few fantasies of her own during the weekend of celebrating her sister. She was happy about the large box of condoms she made sure the hotel provided for her and the other ladies. No way would she be able to pack them in her suitcase for the trip and she needed to be sure there was no suspicion coming from Ray's direction.

Ray was the star of the new Ohio national basketball team, a team that was only two years old and had already won its first national championship, beating out the best of the best teams. The world was still talking about the thirty million a year for four years that Ray was able to get when he agreed to leave the number one team and join the new Ohio squad, making Ohio one of the few states with more than one national basketball team.

She'd met Ray at a pool party hosted by another player the night he'd signed his contract. One of her best friends was an exotic dancer who had been contracted to perform at the all-star party and when Torrie got the call asking if she'd be her plus-one, she wouldn't dare turn down the opportunity. She had spent a few years while in college as a professional cheerleader and dancer for a professional football team, so being around players wasn't foreign to her.

In preparation for the party, she shopped for the sexiest bathing suit that complimented her sexy body. She had ass for days, as she was often told and her natural d-size breasts sat high and luscious on her chest thanks to her daily workout routine which was required as a member of a professional football team cheerleading squad. Even though she gave that up after graduation and now served as an executive for a finance company, she still stayed in shape.

Thanks to her body and her intelligence to not only operate on her sexiness, she was approached by men often, especially those in a professional arena and she could have her pick of any she wanted, but that night, she had eyes for Ray. He was massive in stature at over six feet in height and the length she saw that night between his legs made him out to be the man to meet. She had no qualms about admitting she was in search of good cock that night.

The party that night had been wild and the moment she got the chance to shed her bathing suit and sample his cock, she did and rode him like a professional horse rider. They fucked for over an hour and he turned her in so many positions, she would go from one to the other with one shattering orgasm after the other. Until him, she didn't realize how many times she could multi-climax at a time.

Her relationship with Ray was a good one, though his schedule kept them apart often. Thankfully she wasn't the jealous type to chase him around the country to be sure he wasn't lacing his bed with a different woman every night. She knew what those players did and if Ray decided to indulge, he was smart enough to strap up and never bring anything home. Unbeknownst to him, she had her own sexual proclivities and didn't have time to waste on what he was doing when they weren't together. They loved each other, but the sex had dwindled over time, especially during the heat of the basketball season. Luckily, she knew how to handle her shit and did it with ease without Ray knowing anything about it.

Tonight, she spied a temptation she knew she wanted to sample the moment he stepped in the room. The guys were having fun eating, drinking, dancing and making sure each woman was having the time of her life without limits. There were no cameras allowed and thankful for the kind of money the suite bought, the windows were the kind you could see out, but no one could see in so they were able to enjoy the dark of night filled with a starry sky and not have any worries of their secrets making it into any media outlet.

"Torrie, get your fine ass over here and help take some of these guys off of my hand," Natalie said, dancing and grinding between two dancers. Somewhere along the evening, she had shed the dress she was wearing and she was now in a bright yellow bikini. That was her sister.

"Alright guys, I think up next we have King who's going to entertain us," Torrie said. She couldn't wait because he was the one she had her eye on all night and she also saw him watching her pretty closely too. The attraction was mutual and instant.

She looked toward the spare bedroom where the men were set up to change and prepare and she took her seat along with the other ladies and waited for him to come out. She'd been waiting to see his moves since the moment he arrived. He held back more than the others and now she was about to get an up close and personal look at him and his moves.

King had shown up wearing jeans that covered

his sexy bowed legs. He had on a black t-shirt that stretched across his massively toned chest and the confident stride of his walk made her legs tremble at the thought of riding him. When they'd first arrived, she escorted them to the room where they could shower, change and get ready to entertain for the entire night. Looking at each one of them, they were well worth the price she paid and she was hearing no complaints from the women. This night was an expense she personally paid for with her own money. Now, she sat back, ready for what she knew would be a good show and from the likes of the room, the women were all having a great time. She did notice that each time she looked around, another of the women were wearing less and less clothing.

One of the other men lowered the lights in the room and put on a slow jam, getting the ladies in the mood. Torrie could barely contain her excitement. She leaned back in the chair in her silver slinky dress with only a barely-there silver thong underneath. With the heat in Vegas, a bra was never needed and she only brought one and it's the one she wore when they arrived.

King entered the room and came front and center right in front of her, grinding, winding and moving his big ass cock right in her face. No way could all of that be him. His cock was long and fatter than any she'd ever had, including Ray. She could see the imprint of the large mushroom head covered in a black satin g-string as it beckoned her to have a lick. She couldn't wait for him to drop it so that she could really get a good look. Torrie didn't have to wait long when her eyes focused on his hand as he stroked his length inches from her face. She was a woman that enjoyed sucking a nice, thick cock and it looks like King had more than enough.

She kept her eyes on his length as King slowly slid the g-string down his powerful, muscular legs and when he stood back up to his full height and began dancing, winding and grinding in front of her again, she wanted more than just a dance. He had the kind of cock that she could suck on every day just for the pleasure of having it in her mouth and feeling its pulse on her tongue.

Startling her, King reached down and picked her up, flipped her around and started grinding his hard cock against her ass as he leaned her forward to brace her hands on the seat of the chair. The other women in the room went wild with claps and cheers. He felt good back there and she had an inkling that he would feel even better inside of her. She wiggled her ass as he ground his hips into her to the sway of the music. Before she could focus on the feel, she felt herself being turned back around and lifted.

King lifted her up as if she didn't weigh anything and held her ass in a tight grip flush up against his hard as rock cock. Getting into the action without any coaxing, Torrie wrapped one arm around his neck pulling him close as she ground her hips into his hardness. She was never one to back down from a big cock and that's what she felt King was offering her when he focused his attention on her, wondering if she was open to more than a little dance and grind. She could read the signs on his face. Yeah, she was.

Grinding slowly to the sexy slow music and the impact of the few drinks she'd already downed, Torrie reached down and slipped one of the straps of her dress down her arm until her breasts were exposed. Moving her chest closer to him, she held her breath when he accepted her challenge and without taking his eyes off of hers, he leaned down, still holding her in his grip and still moving to the music, opened his mouth wide and sucked her large round nipple into his mouth, sucking on it like he was trying to extract milk from it. He used his lips to pull on it as it pebbled to a hard peak in his mouth and then he moved to the other one giving it the same attention. Torrie didn't care that they were in a room full of people. Her sister and friends knew how she got down and she wasn't shy when it came to what she wanted and right now, she wanted a little more King. More was definitely on the menu tonight, she thought.

As things got a little hotter between them, she sighed when King kissed his way up her chest to her neck, nibbling on her along the way.

"You are sexy as hell," he whispered in her ear.

Torrie knew no one else could hear them over the music.

"I've got some of my own thoughts about you as well," she replied, almost stuttering out.

"I hope those thoughts involve me fucking you because that's all I can think about at this moment."

Torrie felt a delicious chill run through her body.

"That is one big cock you have," she said.

"Better to fuck you silly with," King replied, causing her body's temperature to rise.

The thong she had on began to feel moist with her juices. The image of his words alone were about to make her shoot off while he held her. Before she could respond, she felt herself being lifted higher up in the air until her pussy was in direct contact with his mouth. The ladies all clapped and shouted even louder for her to get hers as she looked behind King to see two of the other guys laying a blanket out on the floor behind them. Any words she was about to say got lodged in her throat the moment she felt King's tongue glide up and down her cleanly shaved pussy lips. Getting into the moment, she grabbed his head and ground her hips into his mouth as his tongue went past the barrier of her thong and found the entrance to her pussy. Torrie was in ecstasy as his tongue darted in and out of her slowly hitting all of her pleasure points. She looked around to see the expression on the face of her girls only to see that they weren't paying her and King any attention since the other guys had now joined the groove and were putting on individual shows and lap dances for each of them. That was her key to really enjoy the moment and fuck what anyone thought.

Torrie swung her hands in the air and rode King's tongue as if she was riding a bull in one of her favorite supper clubs back in Ohio. Before she could get more caught up and squirt in his mouth, King slid her slowly down his body, leaned down and laid her gently on the blanket. He continued with his show and she continued enjoying every minute of it.

King ground on her, flipped her over on her stomach, rolled her back over, slid his cock across her face and did more flips and turns, all the while turning her on beyond a point where she'd ever been before. She was beyond horny at this point and the cock she felt rubbing all over her was the only thing that could put the fire out that was burning inside of her. She didn't know it would be possible to be as turned on as she was right now. She needed his cock in her so bad, she was ready to beg him to fuck her right in the middle of the floor.

"Get you some, Torrie!" Natalie screamed.

Torrie laughed knowing her sister meant every word. From the looks of things, it looked like Natalie was about to get a little bit of something of her own. The top to Natalie's bikini was now on the floor as her breasts swung free and one of the dancers was feasting on her while also untying the straps to the bottom of her bikini to divest her of all of her remaining clothing.

"I'm trying to get me some, but King is being a tease," Torrie muttered.

King grinned while spreading her legs wide open. She watched as he slid down her body planting his face smack in the center of her pussy. He feasted on her like she was an all-you-can-eat buffet. King draped her legs over his shoulder and she had already been so turned on that she felt her orgasm creeping up her spine. She tried to prolong what she knew was coming because his tongue felt so good slipping and sliding up in her. He placed the right amount of pressure on her clit as he swirled his tongue around and around. Adding more fuel to the fire, he added three fingers to the mix, inserting them into what was the slippery slope of her pussy. The pressure of his tongue and the insertion of his fingers sent her flying as she came with a force that temporarily blurred her vision. Her orgasm went on and on and in the back of her mind, she could hear the tearing of foil. When her body finally began to calm, she opened her eyes that she'd closed to try and contain the explosive nature of the orgasm and saw King sliding an extra large magnum condom on his cock and she knew what was next. She was more than ready for it too.

With King's attention full on her and her body ready for another orgasm, she opened her legs as

King slid up in between them and without needing any help, he slipped slowly into her body as she gasped at the magnitude of the size of his cock. Torrie had never felt anything so wonderful in her life when she originally thought his big cock wouldn't fit or would be too painful to take in. Her orgasm laid the path for his entry into her body and the fact that he took his time going in and out, allowed her body to prepare for the invasion. He was too big for her to take him fully, but he pushed in and then withdrew, repeating the action over and over again giving her more and more of his huge cock each time.

"Damn, your cock is big and it feels so good. Fuck me," she whispered in his ear and he did. Using his strong and powerful thighs to brace himself, King surged into her with a hard thrust that moved her around on the floor and she luxuriated in the feel of him.

"I told you I wanted to fuck you. This cock was tuned into you the moment I walked in the door," King said, stroking into her over and over, giving her what he knew she wanted and felt like she needed.

"Yes!" she uttered riding his cock as he pumped into her slowly making sure she felt every single inch. Her hips rose and fell to meet him stroke for stroke.

"This ten inches is for you and you only. Your body was calling for it. Does that mean there isn't some guy back at home taking care of this sexy pussy on a regular?" King grunted out every word with every push into her body.

"Not like this," Torrie moaned and meant it. Ray gave her good cock, but King was throwing incredible cock in size and motion and her world was officially being rocked.

"What do you say we take this fucking to a more private spot and really let loose?" he said, still fluidly stroking into her.

"Hell yes!" she exclaimed as she felt herself being lifted in the air as he stood with her in his arms and still connected to her intimately. She continued bouncing up and down on him while he walked in the direction of the bedrooms.

Luckily he knew how to walk and fuck because he held her tight while she bounced up and down on his cock getting everything she needed, driving them both to the brink. While she moaned and bounced on his hard cock, she pointed him in the direction of her room. Once inside, King placed her on her feet and turned her around so that she faced the bed.

"Shit!" she said, loving his take charge attitude.

"Yeah, now let's get to some real fucking," he said, right before sliding her thong down her legs and spreading them, widening her stance.

Torrie placed her palms flat on the bed and braced herself for what was next.

"I'm ready."

"So am I," he said.

King pressed her back down and once he did, he grabbed his cock in his hand, spread her cheeks and pointed his cock right at her entrance to her pussy and pushed forward to the hilt. The force made her exhale in delight.

"Yes, fuck me hard just like that," she screamed.

"Oh, you like it hard and rough huh? Tell King what's your pleasure."

"I like it hard, rough and as deep as you want to go, so fuck me, big boy," she crooned saucily.

King didn't need any more encouragement as he grabbed her hips and pumped into her, giving her every inch as the sound of his front slapping against her ass electrified the air in the room.

Torrie was grateful for the music which covered her screams. She was getting fucked like never before. The motion of King's hips and the feel of his cock was everything she'd ever wished for when getting fucked and he was giving her one hundred percent of what he had. She was happily taking everything he was giving her, pushing back into his rolling hips.

"This pussy is so succulent and tight and I knew it would be. Is it good for you?" he asked, still stroking her relentlessly.

"Yes, I love it. Give me more!" Torrie screamed.

King pulled out, flipped her around and stretched her out on the bed. He climbed up with her and grabbed her ankles. Without any pretense,

King draped her legs high up on his broad shoulders, pushing her knees until they were up near her head and pushed his cock deep into her.

"Is this what you want?" he asked, breathlessly.

"Yeah, this is it. Give it to me. Fuck me King," Torrie moaned as she begged over and over for more.

King was pounding into her without pause as she felt another powerful orgasm flowing through her body. King had her legs so high up, if she looked down, she could probably see her own pussy.

"You want it?"

"Yes, I want it all," she exclaimed just before she came with a force that had her trying to leap off of the bed. This orgasm went on and on so long and King continued to pound into her giving her everything she needed. As she pumped up meeting him stroke for stroke, sweat poured off of his head onto her and she saw his face turn up and knew his own release was within reach. Adding to the moment, she gripped his cock with her pussy muscles and that sent him flying over the edge as he grunted out his own orgasm, throwing his head back and growling like a wild animal. The action and watching him caused another orgasm to slam into her as her body moved wildly under him on the bed. Her head pounded to the rhythm of King pounding over and over into her body as they flailed about on the bed together riding out what was the best orgasm of her life.

3 – What Happens in Vegas

Torrie woke up to find King still in bed with her. There was no way she was going to kick him out of her bed after the night of sex they had. He fucked her over and over throughout the night to the point that she didn't even want to go to sleep. After three rounds of wild sex, they went back out and joined the party only to find her sister and two of the other girls had also disappeared into their rooms with other men and according to Alyssa, Natalie had disappeared into her room with two guys. She knew Natalie was getting her life on and that's what the whole weekend was about.

While King slept quietly, she got up and headed for the shower. She could feel how sticky her legs were with the many times she'd climaxed throughout the night. The man was every woman's fantasy and he didn't disappoint. She'd never come so many times with any man before in the same session. She was a wildcat pretty much begging him to take her over and over again. King had a stamina that was unmatched to any man she'd ever encountered, even the few side pieces she had when Ray was on the road and she needed a cock fix.

Torrie turned the shower on, grabbed her favorite shower gel and got in the shower and closed the door behind her. She squirted shower gel on her hands and rubbed it all over her body, closing her eyes and remembering what it felt like to have King's hands all over her. There wasn't a place on her body that he hadn't kissed or felt up and the remembrance had her body feigning for more. The force of his powerful strokes resonated in the aches she felt between her legs and to her, it was the best kind of ache to have. The time she'd paid for them to cater to her and the girls had come and gone and he was still in her bed and she wanted more of his big cock.

Thoughts of what he'd done to her the night before had her sliding her hand down her body to the apex of her thighs. Using the slipperiness of the shower gel, she slid her fingers between her pussy lips and caressed her clit until it turned into a hard nub under her strokes. Torrie closed her eyes and thought of King and his big cock, causing her to insert first one and then two fingers inside her pussy as she ground her hips to a rhythm she remember from the night before. Jolting her, the shower door slid open and before her stood King, still naked with his cock hard as a rock and already covered with a condom.

"You started without me?" he said before stepping into the shower with her.

"You were sleeping soundly," she said reaching out and moving her hands around and over his muscled pecks.

"I'm never sleeping too hard for pussy. I woke up wanting to fuck you and imagine how hard my cock got when I walked in here and found you finger fucking yourself. That was a turn-on. Can I help?" he asked moving closer poking her with his cock.

Torrie didn't say a word as she turned around, planted her hands solidly on the wall and stuck her big ass out at him. King got the message as he stepped between her opened legs and finding the opening to her pussy, he slid into her causing them both to sigh as if they'd been waiting for this connection for a lifetime.

"There is something about your pussy that I can't seem to get enough of," he said sliding up into her from behind.

"Mmmmm, I feel you and every time you touch me, all I can think of is how much more I want. I need more," she mewed.

"I enjoy fucking you. This pussy calls to me in a way none other has and you're wild which is always a plus, so brace yourself for a good pounding just like you like."

Torrie did as he asked knowing he wouldn't let her down and he didn't. King fucked her against the shower wall until she screamed his name as she came over and over.

**

"Ray, I told you she went shopping with one of the girls this morning and she left her phone here which is why I answered it. I don't think she knew she left it, but I'll have her call you when she gets back. She should be back by noon."

Torrie walked into the living room and overheard Alyssa talking on her cell phone to Ray. She left King in the room getting dressed as she went in search of the other girls. Alyssa hung up her phone just as she walked up to her.

"That was Ray?" Torrie asked.

"Yeah it was. I heard this phone ringing and didn't realize it was yours until I answered it and it was Ray. I told him you were out shopping since clearly I couldn't tell him you were getting fucked in the shower this morning. That may not be a good conversation to have with him right now," Alyssa said laughing.

"Girl, I can't get enough of King's cock. He has turned me completely out."

"I saw how big it was and after coming out once to join the party and you disappeared with him again, I figured I wouldn't see you again until the morning."

They walked into the kitchen to see what they could scrounge up and were happy to see trays of fruit in the refrigerator that they never did take out from the night before once the chef cooked up everything and left before the festivities began.

"I would have been up and out earlier, but he brought that big cock into the shower with me this morning and my body had a mind of its own. What about you? Did you get you some last night? I won't tell Todd?" Torrie said playfully, making reference to Alyssa's husband who was back home in Ohio.

"Trust you were not the only chick up in here last night getting her life on. I snatched up the one named Knight Rider and rode his cock all night long."

Torrie gave her a high-five and was glad to know they were all having a good time. Alyssa and her sister Angel were the only two of their group who were married, but married life wouldn't keep them from indulging when they got a chance to. Keeping each other's secrets are what friends are supposed to do and that's what they did.

"What about my sister? Is Natalie up?"

"Girl, your sister is the freak of all freaks. She disappeared into her room with two guys and that bed squeaked and headboard banged all night long. She got her life last night and early this morning. The guys left about an hour ago while you were getting pounded in the shower after they serviced her again this morning. If this is how the rest of our weekend is going to be, I hope we survive!" Alyssa laughed.

"Right. This is only the beginning, though any other cock anyone gets the rest of the weekend is on them. I did the hook up the first night only. What about the other girls? Did they have as much fun as we did?"

"Yeah, we did!" Angel said from behind them as she entered the kitchen.

"Everybody?" Torrie asked.

"Oh yeah, everybody and when I left to take my party into my room, Dyanna was splayed out on the sofa with her legs wide open and all I could see was a guy's head going up and down licking her pussy from here to eternity. Kim, Rina and Paris gave up that ass last night too. Girl, where did you get these studs?"

"I have a couple of stripper friends who referred me to them and I can't speak for them all, but King was worth the investment in the show and especially the extra," Torrie explained.

"They brought exactly what I needed last night. You paid for the show and I got a whole lot more. It's good having friends like you!" Angel exclaimed.

"Right! Sure is," Dyanna said coming into the room.

"Look who came up for air!" Torrie said.

"Yeah, yeah. I needed to soak in the tub first. That guy gave this pussy a workout last night. Speaking of guys, King is in the living room looking for you. I think he's about to leave."

Torrie sat the glass of orange juice she was drinking down on the counter and went to say goodbye.

"So you're leaving huh?" she said walking up to him.

"Thank you for a fun night and morning," King said, pulling her to him and kissing her deeply.

"I'm sorry to keep you beyond your time. If I owe the agency more money for the extra time, let me know"

"You don't. You paid for the show which we gave you. Everything else was because I wanted to and I hope you got what you needed and wanted," he said.

"I got more than I could have imagined," she admitted.

"Well, I live here in Vegas and here's my direct number," he said handing her a card with his personal number scrawled on the back.

"I'm only here for two more days," she said. She wondered if he had time to hook her up again before she left. That would top her weekend off nicely.

"If you find you have time to squeeze in a visit with me all you have to do is either call or text me and say 'More'. No pressure. I won't pester you and I'll wait on. If I don't hear from you, it was nice meeting you and even nicer fucking you. I want to do so again, but remember, that call is up to you."

Torrie didn't know what to say. She paid for the strippers to put on a show and nothing else. She hoped she hadn't paid for what came after or that he was looking to be paid, if by chance she wanted to indulge. He'd definitely taken the sex game a few levels up, but she wasn't willing to pay for that and didn't know how to bring the subject up. Perhaps, she should just stay silent and let him leave and not embarrass herself.

"I had a good time," she said, ignoring his invitation and feeling and probably looking a little uncomfortable. Thoughts of what occurred in the shower and the night before invaded her mind, but how would she say she wanted more, but what did getting more mean.

"Torrie, I see that pretty little mind of yours working overtime and I don't want you to think too hard about this. I enjoy being with you and I know you enjoyed it as well. I don't usually get attached to women when I do a show and I usually try to avoid that, but I like you. You were fun and while I know you are wondering if I'm soliciting you for anything financial, I'm not. I'm not about that. I had sex with you because I wanted to and for no other reason and my desire to do so again is because I want to and I know you want to. Like you said, you're here for two more days and for two more days I want to give you as many more orgasm as that sexy body of yours can handle. No catch, no scheme, no ulterior motive. I'm talking about two days of mind blowing sex and then you can go back to your life. Now, I'm getting out of here because even though I love the night life and exotic dancing, I run a business during the day and I have meetings to get to."

Torrie looked at him and didn't know what to say. She was stunned. This wasn't about any money; this was all about the incredible sex they had and it was out of this world good. She'd be a fool to not want more, but she wouldn't answer now.

"We could do a lot of damage with two days left. Remember, call or text and one word is all you need," King said, before leaning down and planting a killer kiss on her that held the promise of more.

"One word," repeated.

"One word," King said.

When her mind cleared and she could think straight again, he was gone and she was left standing in the doorway with his business card in her hand and her body screaming for his attention as her mind screamed for more!

4 – What Happens in Vegas

"Alright girls. We are in our sexiest attire and let me just say, if I wasn't straight, I'd be all over Torrie in that killer white shift of a dress. Is that even considered a dress or just a long version of a t-shirt," Rina said as they walked into the nightclub.

"She might get us all arrested she looks so hot!" Natalie exclaimed.

"Don't hate 'cause I got the goods!" Torrie laughed as all eyes turned to them.

"This place is jumping! How did you find it?" Natalie asked looking around and hearing congratulations from people as they walked by since she was wearing another sash with the word bride across it.

"A friend of Ray's told me it was the most popular spot in Vegas. There are three locations and all are packed like this, every night."

Torrie looked around and had to agree that it was nice. It was packed with people dancing and drinking and seeing several roped off areas, she noticed a few actors and a few artists she knew whose music was at the top of the charts. This was definitely the place to be.

"Let's get into the mix," Kim said walking away from them and heading straight for the dance floor.

"I have a V.I.P area reserved for us. Give me a minute to check us in before we scatter," Torrie said to Kim before she got too far off. With the size of the club, she'd have a hard time finding her again.

After checking in, Torrie followed one of the hostesses as she led them to their reserved area which was draped in shades of purple, which were the colors for Natalie's wedding party. There was food setup and a private bar area just for them.

"Everything is on the house for you ladies tonight. You can drink in the bar in your private area or go to any of the four bars around the club and hand them one of these chips and they'll know your entire night is free flowing," the hostess said before turning around to leave.

"I'm planning to drink the night away, but I want to dance first, so I'm heading for the dance floor," Angel screamed over the noise of the club.

"I'm going with you," Torrie added. Everyone else followed along.

"Torrie moved to the music as one guy after

another fought his way to dance with her. She danced, grinded, dropped down and swayed to the music, loving the atmosphere. At first she and the ladies stayed close to one another until this man or that man pulled one or the other away.

"Hello beautiful," a voice whispered in Torrie's ear causing her to jump nervously. It couldn't be, she thought. Turning quickly she looked into the face of the man who fucked her silly all night long. Her body recognized him too as she tingled in every intimate place.

"King!" she said leaning into him.

King pulled her into his embrace and kissed her softly on the cheek.

"It's me in the flesh gorgeous."

"What are you doing here? How did you know I'd be here?" she asked curiously.

"You think I'm following you?" King asked.

"No, of course not. Some coincidence running into you here."

A nice coincidence she thought. The minute she heard his voice, her body reacted to the sound of it as it tingled reminding her of the wild night they'd spent together.

"I don't know if I'd say coincidence."

"Is this a place you come to often? It's definitely a happening club. When I checked into a club before coming to Vegas, every single person I asked who had been here told me I needed to come here or to one of the other two locations and now I see why it's considered the hottest club in Vegas."

"It is pretty hot and thanks for the compliment."

Torrie looked at him and wondered why he would thank her for complimenting the club. Maybe it was the Vegas way, she thought.

"Did I just compliment you?" she asked.

"No, you complimented my club," he said, now moving to the music with her in his arms.

"Wait, you own this club?"

King nodded yes.

"Surprised?" he asked.

"Wow, you are just full of surprises. Everyone talks about this place and the other two locations. Do you own all of them?"

"Yes, I do along with three of my partners. We rotate running and overseeing each location along with two gyms and four restaurants, two family spots and two very high-end that are frequented by the rich and famous and anyone else who can afford to pay the price. I also own the company you called to book your dancers for last night."

"Wow."

There was definitely more to King than just a handsome face, a gorgeous body and a big ass cock, she thought, though all had her wondering how she could get a repeat of the night before.

"What? Because I danced for you last night, you thought that was all there was to me? A dancer with a big cock?" he whispered in her ear.

Torrie felt bad and excited at the same time

when he said the word cock. Her mind went right to his.

"I'm sorry. That's not what I meant to insinuate."

King smiled and she felt better.

"Don't worry about it beautiful. Are you and your friends having a good time?"

"Yes, we are. We are really living it up in Vegas and thanks to you, the weekend started out great and has continued again thanks to you and this fly ass club," she said looking around.

"Well, I hope I get to be a part of some of the rest of the time you have left here," King said, still hoping to entice her into letting him get in between her legs again.

Torrie thought about his words and didn't want to admit the number of times she thought of texting or calling him throughout the day.

"I hope so too," she whispered in his ear when he leaned down.

"Well, you know how to reach me and you know what to say. I saw you enter and wanted to come down to say hello. I have a club to oversee and some work to get done in my office upstairs," he said pointing to the glass enclosure on the top level that overlooked everything.

"I'm glad you came down to say hello."

"Well, if you want more than a hello, you know what to do."

Before he left, King reached down, took her hand

and placed it over the center of his cock, making sure no one could see what he was doing and thanks to the darkness of the club, he knew they couldn't. The moment was just for her.

Torrie's next words caught in her throat at the feel of him against the palm of her hand vibrating and growing harder the longer she stood there.

King leaned down to her ear again.

"Just say 'more' and that's all the incentive I'll need," he said and then turned and walked away after planting one last kiss on her cheek. That kiss enflamed her face. She wanted him bad.

Torrie stood in a heap of desire as she watched him walk away flanked by two huge guys with the word security written across the front of their shirts. As people danced around her, her eyes followed King until he turned a corner as was out of sight.

"Torrie, was that King from last night that I just saw you talking to?" Natalie asked, walking up to her.

Gathering herself and getting her mind and body back in check, Torrie wondered how she would survive knowing how close by he was and all she had to do was text or call him and say one word. Her body still tingled from the brief touch of her hand to his cock. The moment her fingers encountered his hardness through his pants, she knew she wanted him inside of her so that she could get back to that feeling of pure satisfaction the minute he entered her and the exuberance she knew she would feel the moment her body vibrated with a body rocking orgasm. She had to shake it off. She couldn't indulge with him again. To her the night before was suppose to be the one and only time and she was supposed to move on. Tonight, encountering him, she was finding that hard to do. She could almost feel his cock's imprint on her hand. She cleared her throat and her mind when Natalie called her name again.

"Torrie?"

"Oh, yes that was him," she said.

"What's he doing here? Hanging with his big cock slinging friends from last night?" she asked.

"Umm, no, he actually owns this spot and the other two locations. Can you believe that? Wait, and he also owns the company I called to book the dancers for last night. Here I thought he was just another exotic dancer with killer fucking skills. That man knows what to do with that big cock of his."

"Damn, he's balling?" Natalie asked.

"I should have known he was more than just a dancer and besides being an incredible lover, he and his partners also own a couple of gyms and restaurants. He's balling big time and in more ways than one," she said slyly, looking at Natalie with a sinister grin.

Natalie looked at her sideways.

"I know that look Torrie. Go do you girl!"

"Oh, I can't. We're here to party and the night

has just begun."

"Sis, look at me. Do I look like I'm not having a good time? I'm having the best time and I'm about to go get me a drink and get this ass back out on the dance floor. I've already seen a couple of guys I'd like to know a little better, if you know what I mean. Trust, I will have no problem getting me some and I don't want you thinking you have to babysit me."

"You sure you don't mine? I mean, I'm not saying I'm going to leave with him or anything."

"Sis, the party is on and I'm about to hit the dance floor again. Go do you. We're here for a fun weekend and that fun isn't just for me, but for you too. Clearly you had a good time with him last night and from the look on your face I see right now, you want a little more. Go ahead, do you. We'll be here for hours, so you have hours to take your time riding that stallion," she snickered and walked off.

Torrie was left standing and contemplating her next move. All around her people danced, grinded, drank and partied and she stood in the middle of them with her pussy throbbing. She did what her sister said and decided to have a little fun of her own. She pulled out her cell phone and found King's number that she'd entered in her phone under a pseudonym and typed, 'More'.

5 – What Happens in Vegas

King watched Torrie from his office overlooking the crowded club. He wondered if he'd enticed her enough to take a trip on the wild side and accept his invitation to revisit the feel of him sliding into her tight pussy, giving her what he knew her body craved. He'd had his share of women, but slipping in between Torrie's legs was heaven on earth. Even now, he had to adjust his cock as it began pressing again the seam of his zipper. He looked down at her from his spot above the crowd through glass that he could see out of, but no one could see in. That was one of the first features he explained to the builder he wanted when construction on the site of the club was discussed. He was glad because no one could see him foaming at the mouth as he ogled her like a peeping-tom from the privacy of his office.

Torrie was not only incredibly beautiful, but sexier than any woman he'd ever met. The moment he saw her and her friends enter his club, he hadn't been able to take his eyes off of her. Unbeknownst to her, he knew who she was, in a relationship with one of the richest ball players in the country. Lucky guy, he thought, as he imagined getting some of her sweet pussy every night and twice in the morning. He couldn't help himself when he decided to go down and say hello. He could have easily let her enjoy her night with her friends and took the night before as a one-night stand, but he couldn't. The way she looked in that little dress had him imagining spreading her out on his desk and eating her pussy until she screamed for him to stop because she couldn't handle another orgasm. The moment the image entered his mind, his cock stood at attention, or as much as it could in his boxer briefs that barely contained his massive size. He wanted to smell her, feel her and especially taste her.

King shifted in his stance as he watched her and thought of all the things he'd like to do to her. He wanted to feel her legs draped over his shoulders as his lips tasted her sweetness over and over. He had a feeling she was uninhibited in her desires especially after the night and morning of incredibly wild sex they'd had. If she was anything like him, and he had a feeling she was, she was more than ready to continue what they started the night before. She only had a day or so left in Vegas and usually he had no problem walking away from one woman and onto the next immediately, but Torrie, he wanted fiercely.

King's desire for her led him to go down to the main floor and approach her with every intention of tempting her into a little rendezvous in his office where they would have the utmost privacy. No one got past his security at the stairs or at the elevator unless he wanted them to get by. The off-duty police he used made sure of that and they also knew what happened in his office, stayed in his office.

He stood watching her as the words he spoke to her wreaked havoc on her thoughts of taking him up on his offer or letting the night before be the beginning and ending. From his vantage point, he could see her thinking it over, but not take any action to reach out to him. King was about to look away when he saw Torrie reach in her bag and pull out her cell phone. She took her time typing something and the minute she was done, his cell phone buzzed on his hip and he smiled.

King took out his phone and saw her one word message and knew she was about to make his night, again. He typed back instructions telling her to come up to his office. He told her to come toward the back of the club where she'll see two guys standing at the elevator. They'll know to punch in the code for the elevator to go up and he'd be waiting for her on the other side.

As soon as Torrie read his message and he saw her walk toward the back, he sent a text to his security detail at the elevator to let her up.

King looked around his office straightening a few things up before once again adjusting his rock hard cock and went in search of her. As he reached the elevator where additional security was standing on his level, he waited only a few seconds before the doors opened and out stepped Torrie in all of her beauty in that killer ass white mini-dress.

"Why don't you guys take an hour break," he told his security before escorting Torrie into his office and locking the door behind them.

"Well, hello again beautiful," he said.

Torrie looked at him and was drawn to his hot body and delectable handsome face. He reminded her of her favorite actor, Omari Hardwick. To her, the actor was the finest man she'd ever seen and King could be his twin, though he was a little darker in complexion, which she loved. Nothing turned her on more than a hot, chocolate brother. Being white, she'd always had a thing for black men and friends often teased her by calling her a Kardashian whom everyone knows about their love black men and Torrie couldn't blame them.

"Hello again to you too. I hope you were expecting me to respond to your invitation," she said, walking over and looking out over the entire club floor.

"I sure was hoping so."

"This place is incredible and this office is amazing. You can see everything from here."

King walked up behind her, making sure to rub his cock across her fat ass. He wanted her to know he wasn't playing when he said he wanted her. His words still rang true from the night before when he said he wanted to fuck her and tonight was no different.

"I could see you from here and I could see how delectable your tits looked in this dress. I found myself imagining this dress dropping from your body so that I could see you in the flesh," he said leaning down and placing an opened mouth kiss along the slope of her neck.

Torrie moved her head to the side to give him access to as much of it as he wanted. His mouth felt hot and wet as he nipped and licked at her neck. She moaned, loving the attention and squirmed when she felt his big, strong hands come up and over her hips on a path to her breasts. She leaned back into him as he lightly caressed her tits through her dress.

"Your hands are magical," she crooned, right before she felt him turn her face so that he could capture her lips in a searing, penetrating kiss. The first touch of his tongue to hers had her ready to hike her dress up and spread her legs wide for him to dispense with any foreplay and just fuck her.

"I have another magical tool if you're up for it," he whispered against her lips.

"Won't someone see us?" she asked, hesitantly.

"No one can see us. This glass is made for me to see out and not allowing anyone to see in, just like the windows on your hotel suite. No one will know what goes on up here except for you and me and right now, I need some pussy and the way your ass is moving against my cock, I'd say you're ready for that pussy to get another work over like last night," he crooned in her ear.

"Don't forget about his morning in the shower," she added, turning around to face him.

King took her bag from her and and placed it on the top of the bar in his office. Not taking his eyes off of hers, he leaned down and captured her lips again in a kiss that was even hotter than the one they'd just shared. At the same time, he reached down and pulled her dress up over her hips so that it was up around her waist. When he ran his hands across the fat globes of her ass, he realized she wasn't wearing any panties and his excitement for her went up a few more notches. He pulled back from the kiss and looked into her eyes before leaning down to her ear.

"Oh, you are nasty and I love it. No panties tonight. What were you expecting to get into or to get into you?" he moaned in her ear. Before she could answer, he sucked her earlobe into his mouth.

"Nothing until you showed up," she said, sighing as she experienced an erotic haze.

"I love a woman who likes to come out with no panties on. That makes it easier and less work for me to slide my cock in. Are you ready for that?" he murmured while reaching in front of him to undo his belt and zipper to let his pants slide to the floor. He stepped out of them as he watched Torrie pull her dress over her head and completely off of her body.

"I hadn't figured on running into you and getting another ride on this cock," she said reaching out to stroke his hard cock through his briefs. Over half of his cock couldn't stay under the band of his underwear he was so long, hard and thick.

"I guess I'm the luckiest man in this place tonight," King said.

"You and I both. You have no idea how glad I am," she admitted before laying her dress neatly across the top of the bar on top of her purse. Before King could say anything, she slid down to her knees, sliding his underwear down his legs, keeping her eyes on him as she dipped her head and sucked the head of his cock into her mouth. She had to open her mouth wide to take in the huge tip.

"Damn!" King said between his now clinched teeth. Torrie's mouth felt good on his cock and that was one act they never did get to the night before, but he was glad it was on her agenda tonight.

"I wanted a taste of this big boy last night, but you couldn't seem to get enough of getting in my pussy and I never got around to it."

King struggled to get the words out as Torrie quickly did away with his boxers sliding them all the way down and off of his body. Before he could get a word out, he watched as half of his cock disappeared into her mouth, catching him off guard, not giving him a chance to prepare for the assault her mouth was planting on his cock.

Torrie sucked cock like she loved it and it was her favorite part of sex. She loved the feel of a hard, throbbing cock on her tongue and King had plenty for her to taste. There was no way she would be able to get it all in her mouth, but she took in as much of him as she could get.

"That's it baby, suck it. Shit, Torrie, you are doing that!" he exclaimed, watching her head bob back and forth and all around showing him how much she was enjoying giving him head.

"Mmmm," she moaned, sending vibrations from his cock and through his body.

King didn't want to hurt her, but he loved a woman on her knees in the perfect position for him to watch what she was doing and to also lend to the act. He placed one hand on her head and entwined it with the long blond tresses of her hair as he helped guide her mouth up and down on his cock the way he liked. Each time she took him in a little further until she practically gagged, something that didn't seem to bother her at all. Each time she took him deep, he could feel her relaxing the muscles at the back of her throat to give him even more pleasure. King pumped slowly into her mouth until he saw a look in her eyes that said she wanted more.

"More?" he asked and with the nod of her head, he surged forward, adding a little more power to his strokes. She lapped at him, sucked him and in between, licked her way up and down his shaft. He was so hard, his cock felt like it would explode on its own. He was about to burst, but wanted to hold on to it.

Torrie was about to complain when King slipped his cock out of her mouth and stood her up.

"Don't fret sugar. I know you like blowing me, but right now, I need to get another taste of this pussy that has been haunting me all day. I don't just want a sample of your sweetness like I got last night. Tonight, I want you laid out like a buffet for me to get all I can eat."

Torrie shrieked when King lifted her from her feet and planted her ass on the top of his desk. He pushed her legs wide open, slid down to his knees in front of her and before she could register the impact of what he was about to do, he went right in without any pretense.

King captured her clit between his teeth and nipped lightly before lapping the nub back and forth with his tongue. Torrie immediately started grinding her hips into his face as he pulled her closer to the edge. Using first one and then two fingers, he spread he pussy lips and inserted his fingers inside. He grinned when he saw Torrie throw her head back and tried to prevent the scream that he knew she needed to release.

"Let it go, baby. No one is going to hear you over the club music noise. Scream as loud as you want to."

Torrie rode King's tongue like she was riding for her life. She used one hand to grip the desk and used the other to place it on his head letting it follow the movements as he eat her pussy like a starving man. He sucked on her clit, while his fingers fucked her as her juicy essence coated his fingers and caused a ring around his lips.

"You taste incredible," he said, right before diving back in.

Torrie thought she would leap off the table the moment he used his tongue to fuck in and out of her, driving her to a powerful orgasm, which she knew he could do over and over. She tried to prepare herself for what was coming, but couldn't. Her orgasm hit her like a truck and she came hard right on his tongue. She screamed as King lapped at her pussy over and over until her body stopped shaking and quivering. Just when she thought she was sated, she heard the sound of a condom wrapper and before she could open her eyes to look beyond the stars that had formed behind her eyelids, King's hard cock was at the entrance to her pussy, ready to plunge inside. If she wasn't ready, she knew she needed to be because if her memory served her correctly, she was really in for a ride now.

King leaned forward, taking Torrie's lips in a heated kiss, letting her taste her own pussy on his lips as he pushed forward with his hips and slid his cock inside of her juicy, wet pussy. He loved the feel of her gripping him tight with her pussy walls and when he began to rock into her hard, grinding and circling his hips, he allowed his tongue to fuck her mouth the way his body was fucking her below.

Torrie joined in the act by planting her hands flat on the desk and raising her hips to join in the rhythm of their fuck session. Before long, she felt her body's temperature rise as another orgasm lingered on the horizon. His cock felt so good, she was already on the brink of a second orgasm.

"I'm about to come again," she breathed into his mouth.

"I'm right with you baby," King said, now surging into her body, chasing his own orgasm that was threatening to send him into convulsions. As soon as Torrie screamed out her pleasure and shattered into a million pieces in his arms, King joined her as he felt himself coming along with her. He gripped her hips tight and slammed into her body over and over, riding out the wave of pleasure he knew he would experience once he got inside of her. He pumped until Torrie held onto him, afraid she'd collapse back on the table.

"Shit!" she sighed.

"I got you, sugar," he said holding on to her while his body calmed from the explosion.

When he could breathe again and knew he wouldn't collapse from having no blood in any part of his body, he leaned back, found her lips and kissed her with a deep kiss that was filled with gratitude for giving and taking from him at the same time and in turn, making his head spin from the sheer magnitude of what they'd just experienced together.

"I can't tell you how much I needed that," she said.

"Woman, you are trying to kill a man. This here is some good, delicious and succulent pussy and I'm glad you enjoy fucking me as much as I enjoy fucking you. As soon as I saw you walk into the club, my cock got hard and zoomed right in on you and once again, well worth it," he said kissing her again.

"Right back at you. You are one irresistible man," she said, lowering her legs to the desk as King stepped from in between them to remove the condom.

"Stay right here," he said and walked away into what was a room connected to his office. She looked closer into where he went and noticed the room was in fact a bedroom. In a few short seconds, he returned with a warm wash cloth for her.

"You sleep here?" she said, making reference to the bedroom.

"Some nights I do when I'm too tired to go home. There's a full loft apartment back there. If you want to go into the bathroom to wash up better, go ahead. I left a towel for you on the bathroom counter. You are extremely juicy tonight," he quipped.

Torrie laughed along with him.

"That's all because of you and that good cock," she said coming down from the table and walking in the direction that he'd come from.

"You have ass for days, sexy."

Torrie switched harder and looked back at him over her shoulder. She walked into the bathroom and washed off the traces of the two powerful orgasms King had given her.

"To think, all it took to get some of that cock again was one little word, more," she said and smiled. She knew this was going to be a weekend she'd never forget.

6 – What Happens in Vegas

"Last night was so much fun," Rina said as they all gathered for a late breakfast.

"It was, especially after Torrie returned all sexed up. I think I even noticed her walking funny. I take it King hit you off right again," Natalie said.

"That he did and then some," Torrie said.

"What was all that howling coming from your suite this morning, Natalie?" Kim asked, sampling some of everything their personal chef for the weekend had cooked up and left for them.

Natalie tried to ignore them until they heard a noise behind them and the howler entered the room.

"I have to get going. I had fun last night and this morning. Congratulations on the wedding and you know where to find me if you're ever in Vegas again. Hello ladies," he said acknowledging them all before turning and walking out of the suite.

When Natalie turned around, all eyes were on her.

"I swear, our men are never going to be enough if we don't learn to stay away from cock on the side. Who was that?" Torrie asked.

"That, ladies, was our resident howler," she laughed.

"Well, we got that. Where did he come from?"

"I met him at the club last night and he gave me his number. After I got back here and all of you finally crashed, I had an itch I needed scratching so I invited him over and he had pipe for days. I don't even know if that howling was him or me!" she said doubling over laughing. Everyone else laughed with her.

"Well, I see I'm not the only one who got her freak on last night," Torrie said, reliving her time with King in his office the night before.

"Oh, it wasn't just you and me. I heard some noises coming from Paris' room sometime last night too. What gives Paris?" Angel said.

Paris blushed, attempting to ignore them, but knowing they would never allow that.

"Oh that? That was Krissy. I met her at the club last night and she had a tongue that should be registered as a lethal weapon because she killed this pussy in the early hours."

Everyone looked at Paris with shocked faces. None of them knew that Paris liked women, but they were all getting their life on since arriving in Vegas, so why should Paris be any different, Torrie thought.

"Well, get yours Paris. I ain't mad at you!" Natalie said.

"It was buckets of fun," Paris said.

"I'm just glad we're all having fun and not just being about entertaining me. This is a weekend for us all to let our hair down. What are you going to do tonight by yourself after we all leave this evening?" Natalie asked.

Torrie had booked an extra night for herself since Ray was away and she wanted a relaxing day to just chill. Everyone else was leaving later in the day and she was staying until Monday evening.

"I know what she's going to do," Kim said.

"Yeah, she's going to do King and get her last earth shattering orgasms in before she has to return to her life."

"I know you sluts think that's what I'm going to do, but we said our goodbye's after that last good fuck last night. I'm serious about spending this last night and tomorrow just relaxing. I have to be back to work first thing Tuesday and I need to get my mind back on that."

No one said anything, but none of them believed her. She didn't really believe herself. King was becoming addictive and soon she would be back home with Ray. She knew she needed to stop, but that cock of his brought her pleasure like she'd never, ever known before. She would fight the urge and concentrate on relaxing for her last day.

"Well, let's stop talking about how much of a freak we all are and get out of here. We've got shopping to do and a comedy show this afternoon before our goodbye dinner."

"You're right. This has been a great weekend. Thanks Torrie for planning this weekend for us to let our hair down. This is exactly what I needed," Natalie said and the other ladies chimed in with agreement.

"Anything for my sister!" she said.

"Alright, a few minutes to get dressed and we're out," Natalie said.

**

"King, I stopped by your house this morning to talk about the expansion of the club to the east coast and I couldn't reach you," Darien said.

He and King had been friends and partners since their college days back in Boston where they graduated at the top of their class before moving to Vegas to open up their joint business venture of supplying male exotic dancers to women who traveled to Vegas looking for a good time.

He and King both worked as dancers while in college to supplement money their parents would send them. Soon after, they no longer needed money sent to them and found they were sending money home to their parents.

After graduating, they decided to start their

business in Vegas and after five years, not only had they and two other friends opened up the three clubs, but they also opened up several gyms, restaurants and soon, two high end men clothing stores. Today, he and King were suppose to meet to talk about meetings they were setting up to take their businesses to other parts of the country, expanding the brand.

"King, did you hear me?" Darien said to a distracted King.

King found himself daydreaming. He was going through paperwork in his office when Darien called to see where he was. He showed up when King still had his mind on images of him taking Torrie on his desk and then again on the sofa in his office before she cleaned up and went back down to the club to enjoy her friends. He watched her as she left and as soon as he saw her back on the dance floor, his body hardened for her even though he'd enjoyed two explosive orgasms with her in his office. He was desperate for her, but didn't bother her again, instead letting her enjoy her night out with her sister. He had already monopolized enough of her time.

"Yeah, I heard you. I slept here at the club last night. The place was packed and after Truth showed up to help me count out for the night, we got to talking and drinking and after he left, I was too tired and drunk to drive. Besides, Torrie was here last night and she hit me off a few times here in the office. I swear that woman has pussy that would make a man die a happy, slow death in it and her blowjob skills are off the chain."

"Torrie from the other night? You hooked up with her again?"

"Damn right I did. She came to the club with her crew last night and as soon as I saw her, I knew I was digging up in that before she left and she was just as horny as I was. No way was I going to drive after what she put on a brother," he laughed.

"Dude, don't tell me you are getting sprung on a client."

King looked up at him like he had several heads.

"Stop playing. You know me better than that, but you are no different and you wouldn't pass up pussy and head that good either, so shut it down," he said laughing.

"Yeah, you're right. I guess you're happy you had to substitute when Vinny had to drop out at the last minute the night at her hotel suite."

"I sure am. You know I still love the show and very seldom do I indulge in pussy with clients, but there was something about her because just being around her keeps me rock hard."

"Did she stay with you?"

"No, she left with her crew. They flew back home today, but I think Torrie is still here."

"Didn't you tell me she's the girlfriend of a baller?"

"Yeah, she is. A thirty million dollar baller. It's

that guy, Ray, the best in the league right now."

Darien hit him with a shocked expression on his face.

"Really? Damn, that's crazy. She was all over your cock and she has a thirty million dollar man back at home."

"Hey, thirty million don't make you satisfy a woman in bed. It only satisfies her pocketbook."

"Right. Do you think you'll see her again?"

"Maybe, maybe not. If so, it's on her. I don't stalk, so if she wants this cock, she knows where to find me."

"Alright, well, let's get down to business. I need to fly to Miami this week to start the conversation about the expansion and since you're leading the effort when it comes to the clubs, I need to be sure I have it all together before I'm at the table."

King put his paperwork away and pulled out new papers to go over with Darien. In the back of his mind, he wondered if he would see Torrie again. That was up to her and if so, he'd be ready.

7 – What Happens in Vegas

Torrie walked back into the suite and immediately noticed the quiet now that everyone had gotten on their flight back home. It was indeed a great weekend and she was looking forward to enjoying her last night in Vegas by getting a massage, taking a swim in the indoor heated pool and relaxing. She thought about switching to a smaller suite since she was by herself, but decided against it. She only had one more day.

Walking over to the bar, she made herself a drink and thought through her day of relaxation and after only a few minutes, her thoughts turned to King. She'd been fighting the temptation to call him all day. She knew she wanted him and she wanted him badly.

"Why am I denying myself," she said out loud. There really was no reason. She'd already fucked

King several times and one more night won't make it any worse than the first time. Somewhere in the back of her mind, she waited for regret over her actions to set in, but it never happened. It was just sex and men did it all the time. She didn't know what Ray did when he spent more days on the road than at home and she didn't care as long as he strapped up just as she has every man she fucks to do. She loved sex and she saw no reason to deny herself. With King, she couldn't seem to get enough of him. He had a cock meant to please and she appreciated it.

The evening was still pretty young and the quiet of the room gave her more time to think and make the decision she already knew she was going to make. Turning the water off in the Jacuzzi tub now that it was full, she grabbed her cell phone, found the number she needed and typed, 'more'. Five minutes passed by before she heard her phone beep. Picking it up, she smiled thinking it was King responding, but instead it was Ray.

'Hey, baby!'

'Hi, Ray. Are you getting ready to hit the road?'

She knew the team had an away game and he'd be gone for two weeks, another reason she decided to stay another day. If she had left with the other girls, he would have been gone by the time she got home, so she was in no rush.

'I'm already at the airport. The team is boarding the plane. I wanted to check to be sure

you were okay. Are you ladies having a good time?'

Torrie had to remember to not let it slip that she was in Vegas alone for the last day. Thankfully, none of the ladies would let it slip since they always had each other's back.

'Yeah, we're having a great time. I miss you.'

'I miss you too. Why don't you come join me on the road for a few days?'

'I have a few meetings this week, but the next week is open enough that I can take some time off. If you give Craig an autographed basketball, I'm sure he'll overlook the fact that I would be taking off again after being off the past few days.'

Craig was her boss and she often used perks from Ray to get her way with him and it always worked. Recently he asked her about the possibility of him getting a signed ball.

'I'll make sure he gets signed ball. Anything to get your sweet ass in a bed under me as soon as possible. My cock hurts it needs you so bad.'

'Keep it hard for me baby and I'll take care of you, you know that.'

Torrie jumped when her phone beeped while she talked to Ray.

'You know it. I wish I had time before getting on this plane to have you do a live, sexy show for me. You know how much I love watching you with those legs wide open and that pretty pink pussy all wet and slippery just for me.'

'Let's set a date after your game tomorrow night. I'll be home by then and ready to give you the show of your life.'

'Damn, baby. You know how my I want you and now I have to get on this plane with a hard-on. Have fun and I'll talk to you tomorrow.'

'I love you Ray.'

'Love you too baby.'

Torrie scrolled through and found that King had responded while she was talking to Ray.

'Ready for me?' King had typed.

'Absolutely. I think you're turning me into a nympho. I can't remember being this horny and all the time before I met you.'

'Is that so. Well, tell me a fantasy you have. Tell me something sexy you've always wanted to try, but haven't. This is your last night in Vegas, so let's have some fun.'

Torrie thought about revealing one secret desire she'd never told anyone. This is why she felt like she could never get enough of getting more when it came to sex. King fucked her without a pretense of love or affection, but just gave her exactly what she needed; what her body needed. She could freely enjoy being who she was and that was a woman who loved everything about sex and wanted to explore a wilder side of herself, someone she couldn't be with Ray. She didn't mind good, straight sex, but if she got the chance to try something new that she'd always fantasized about, she was all for it.

'*Well?*' King typed.

She was thinking too hard and too long when King sent another text before she could respond. She went for it.

'*Got a friend?*' she typed back.

Torrie bit her lip in anticipation of what those three words meant.

'*Male or female?*'

'*Male.*'

'*What time?*'

'*Whenever you get here and bring swim gear.*'

'*I'm giving instructions to my team for the club tonight and we'll be there.*'

A chill went through Torrie's body when she saw that he typed 'we'. She was about to experience a first and the mere thought of it had her about to come in the spot where she stood. She felt a quick rush of liquid pool between her legs with the thought of what was about to happen.

**

Torrie relaxed after a taking a hot shower and then a cold one to cool her body's temperate. She was in need worse than an animal. She'd used every bit of strength she had to not pleasure herself to climax because she needed that feeling and instead she waited, trying to keep herself busy until King and his friend arrived. She'd changed from her red bikini to her very sexy pink stringed bikini and turned on the whirlpool in the Jacuzzi when her cell phone rang; it was King.

"I'm in the lobby."

"Give your name to anyone at the check-in counter and they'll give you a card key that you'll need for the elevator to reach this floor."

"Got it."

Torrie looked around to be sure she was ready. She'd ordered food and there was plenty to drink and though she had no doubt King would come with his own condoms, she'd had one of the assistants assigned to her suite to pick up a supply of them for her. She had a feeling it was going to be a long and extremely fun evening. Slipping on a pair of black strappy stilettos to add to her barely-there bikini bathing suit, Torrie headed for the door to let them in. She opened the door to the suite just as the elevator reached her floor and when the doors opened, her mouth hung open when she got a look at King in all of his muscly fineness and then exiting behind him was a god-like specimen that reminded her of what she pictured Hercules would look like. He was tall, hot, sexy and after quick look down his body, he appeared to be just as hung as King.

"Gentlemen," she said greeting them.

King didn't respond. He walked over, pulled her to him and kissed her deeply, going at her mouth like a starving man. When the kiss ended, she was breathing as if she'd just run a marathon. The power-packed kiss spoke volumes to what she knew would be coming next. When he walked past her into the suite, she moved to the side to let his friend in and surprising her, this new friend pulled her into his arms and he too sucked on her lips before diving into her mouth with a tongue that searched out hers and ventured around in her mouth before pulling back and smiling at her like he'd been waiting a lifetime to do that.

"Hello. I'm Zeus," he said.

"Hmm, yes you are," she replied and let him walk by as well.

"I see you're ready for a dip in the Jacuzzi," King said, looking at her like he wanted to devour her and also noticing the Jacuzzi tub full of water that was bubbling from the jet stream system.

"I was hoping the two of you would like to join me."

"Of course. Tonight is whatever you desire," King said.

"In that case, if you'd like to change, pick any of the rooms. I'm going to grab a drink and I'll be in the Jacuzzi when you return."

King and Zeus walked off.

Torrie had been in the Jacuzzi only a few minutes when she looked up to see two of the finest men she'd ever seen standing before her in tiny swim trunks and cocks that didn't fit in them even halfway. She licked her lips knowing what she was in store for.

"Well, it looks like those swimming trunks are a

waste," she said, acknowledging how hard both of their cocks were, standing long, hard and thick against their stomachs.

Without words, both men removed them and stood before her completely naked. King moved first stepping over the ledge and joining her in the Jacuzzi. Zeus moved to join them on the other side. Knowing King was a man of action, she wasn't surprised when he pulled her to him and while taking her lips in a deep, penetrating kiss, he reached behind her and undid the strap to release her breasts into his hands. He pulled back and dipped his head, pulling one hard nipple into his mouth, going between tugging on it, nipping it and then licking it to soothe and caress the tips.

Torrie could die right now from the feeling. It was incredible. There was movement behind her as the water shifted and Zeus stood behind her with his hard cock poking her in the back. She sighed in relief when he dipped down to allow his hard cock to caress the area between her ass cheeks. She ground back against him letting him know she liked what he was doing.

Zeus slid his cock down even further and rubbed the head in between her legs letting her feel the large mushroom head of it as it slid back and forth across her pussy lips. She was more than ready for more. For a better feeling, she felt Zeus slide the bikini part of her bathing suit down her legs and watched as it floated to the top of the water's surface. This time when he slid his cock across her pussy lips, the sensation floated throughout her body.

"You have a hot ass mouth," King said in between deep kisses that were driving her crazy.

"Yes I do."

"I have a need for this hot mouth," he said tracing her lips with the tip of his finger before slipping it into her mouth. Torrie didn't hesitate to lick and suck on it, showing him what she would do if instead of his finger, he'd slide his cock in between her lips. They must be on the same wave length when King moved to sit on the edge of the Jacuzzi so that his crotch was level with her face. She smiled wide when King placed his hands on her head and moved it toward his cock that seemed to be staring right at her. Without too much coaxing, Torrie opened her mouth wide and sucked him in. She didn't do it lightly or slowly, but she opened her mouth and took as much of him in as she could, going all the way down until the tip of his cock pushed up against the back of her throat. Relaxing her throat muscles, she tried to take even more as King pumped into her mouth.

While she was busy going down on King, Zeus, still behind her reached around to the front of her and stroked her pussy lips with his fingers while still grinding his cock into her ass. She felt like she was floating, her body was so wired up from the attention. She could feel them both all over her body as it screamed more, more, more. Without saying it, more is exactly what she got.

Hearing the tearing of a condom, Zeus backed up to slide it on before coming back up, pushing her to lean over a little and surged into her body, sliding his cock all the way into her.

"Yes!" she moaned out loud against King's cock that filled her mouth. The pleasure was so intense, she was finding it hard to concentrate on anything else, but the feel of how long and thick he felt inside of her. She was living out a fantasy, a cock in her pussy and one in her mouth. She continued giving to them as much as they were giving to her. She sucked King harder, hearing his moans of enjoyment and the sound of Zeus grunting with each pump into her pussy was driving her over the edge quickly.

"Suck it, Torrie," King urged her on as he pumped harder and deeper into her mouth. "You love it?" he asked.

Torrie nodded. She more than loved it. She was getting a fantasy fulfilled by two big cocks. What more could a woman ask for. Before she could prepare herself, the double assault was exactly what her body needed, cock filling two holes and the sensation below sent her shattering through a powerful orgasm that rocked her body and traveled from her to King as he exploded in her mouth. Torrie didn't pull back, but lapped up every drop, wanting more and more. She held her head and mouth still as he fucked it good and deep making sure she caught every drop of him in her mouth.

Behind her Zeus grunted even louder as he pounded hard into her just the way she liked. Before long, she felt his hotness fill the condom as he pumped through his release. As her body calmed from the double penetration, King reached down and pulled her up and out of the water. She was still in an erotic fog when she watched him place a condom on his cock which was still rock hard.

"I know you need more, don't you?" he asked.

"Yes," she uttered, not ashamed of her need to be fucked good and always wanting more.

"Good. Come ride me baby," he said.

Torrie crawled over after the condom was in place and threw her leg across his hip as he laid flat on the carpet. She braced her hands on his chest, raised her hips and slid down on his hard flesh, throwing her head back in ecstasy. Torrie rode King like he was the last man on the planet and this was their last sex session together. In essence, it was and she needed to be sure to get all she needed before she headed back to her life.

"You are exactly what I needed for my last day here," she said smiling down at him.

"Tonight is still young," King said as he surged up into her right before they both screamed and climaxed together.

Torrie's last thought before she collapsed on his chest was that she would never be able to think of the word 'more' as just an ordinary word any more. Every time she heard it, she would think of King and her time in Vegas. She now knew that more meant as much as she wanted and she would always want more.

8 – What Happens in Vegas

Six Months Later

"Congratulations, Torrie! I swear, I thought Ray would never propose. I was beginning to question his love for my sister," Natalie said.

"No, don't question that. He has actually proposed to me around five times and I wouldn't accept. I was fine with my life as the girlfriend of a professional ball player, but I had concerns about that turning into me being his wife and the mother of his children. He's on the road so much and he talks about all these kids he wants to have and all I saw was that being all on me. I finally put that reservation to the side and accepted and I'm excited about it."

"Yeah! We have so much to do and plan for. I know you went all out for my girls' weekend in Vegas and my bachelorette party here in town, but of course I'm not rolling in the money like you, but I still want to give you an incredible send-off into marriage. What do you want to do?"

Torrie knew exactly what she wanted to do and she had no problem footing the bill.

"Don't you dare get all worried about money when it comes to plans for any parties for me. I want to do a girl's weekend, preferably to Vegas and the bridal shower here for family and friends is going to be off the chain and I know you think you should pay because I paid for you, but don't you worry about that. I'll pay for everything and I'll let you plan it all down to the last detail. You know you'll have to be my matron of honor and I'm going to ask Rina to be my maid of honor."

Natalie screamed on the other side of the phone.

"I can't tell you how excited I am for you. I wouldn't be anywhere else, but by your side and you know that. Do you want to get together for dinner and drinks this weekend with the girls? Unlike me who got married a year after I got engaged, you're getting married in four months and there is a lot to do. Now, for starters, I assume you want to stay at the same place we stayed for my trip to Vegas or did you have another place in mind?"

"I loved that place and that suite was everything. Everyone had their own room and there were still three rooms left over."

"Okay, I figured as much, but I wanted to be sure while I'm working on details."

Torrie wasn't sure if she should bring up the weekend entertainment, but for her she didn't want any male strippers. She already had her own personal entertainment in mind and knowing how well all the girls could keep a secret, she had no worries about her rendezvous getting out.

"I can't wait to plan some fun stuff. What about entertainment? I have some things in mind, different from my weekend so that we can switch it up, but what about our male entertainers from my weekend?"

Torrie knew Natalie was making reference to King. She hadn't talked to him since she left Vegas. No one had ever made her come as hard or as much as he did and she had to admit he dished up the best sex of her life. She hated comparing him to Ray, but there really was no comparison. She loved Ray, but when she really needed to be hit off right, she knew King had what she wanted and needed and for her girl's weekend, she planned on getting tapped as many times as possible, depending on his schedule and if he were still interested.

"I would say, check with the girls to see what they want, but as for me, I have that covered, I think."

"King?" Natalie asked.

"Yes. Is that wrong?" she asked.

Torrie had never, ever doubted herself or her actions before, but to her, fucking King wasn't hurting anyone and there were some secrets she would take with her to the grave. King was one of those secrets.

It had been six months since she'd last saw or spoke to him and she knew that his clubs were the hottest talk around the country. She'd read someplace that he and his partners were expanding their brand to New York, Miami and Colorado. His gyms were already being opened up in several other markets around the country. He was blowing up and she wasn't sure he still had time to hook up with her. By now, she had no doubt, with his stamina, women were walking on shaky legs and sore pussies on the regular.

"If I thought it was wrong, I would be wrong too."

"Maybe we're both wrong," Torrie said.

"Torrie, you were the one who taught me to love life a little more and just go with what I want to do. You know I'm always telling you the same thing, to do you. What happens in Vegas or anywhere else, you know stays between us. You and I are sisters, but our group of friends know that we never tell each other's business and we cover when needed. If what you want is King when we're in Vegas, do you my sister. Of course, I'll be hooking up some additional fun for the ladies, because that's the only extracurricular fun some of them get to have, afraid to have a little fun on the side when at home. When we're away, it's whatever goes and that weekend won't be any different. I take it you have a way to reach King?"

"That I do and thanks for being my best friend and sister. There is none like you."

"Ditto for me sis. I'll give the ladies a call and tell them we're hanging out this weekend and I'll let you tell them about the engagement. I love you!" Natalie shouted.

"I love you, too."

Torrie hung up and paced around her office. She wondered if she should give King a ring and see if he was still as open to pleasuring her as he had been six months ago.

Throwing caution and doubt out of the window, she picked up her phone and searched for the name "Missy" on her cell phone. In order to keep things under the radar, she created that name for King's number just in case there was ever a chance that Ray would begin questioning her, which she doubted he ever would. Not many men think their women are stepping out, especially the woman of a thirty million dollar man. She loved him, but she needed more and she knew exactly where to get it.

Finding the name "Missy" on her phone, she typed in for letters, M-O-R-E, and waited. A few minutes went by and no response. She then began to question her decision to reach out to him knowing that he may not even remember who she was. Torrie decided to busy herself as she prepared for her meeting and after ten more minutes, checking the clock and noticing the time getting closer to the start of her meeting, she was about to place her cell phone in her purse when it vibrated. She quickly checked it and saw the name "Missy" appear on the screen. She clicked the name to read the message.

'When and where, Torrie?'

Torrie shrieked with excitement.

'Vegas, same suite one month from today. I will be in Las Vegas that weekend celebrating my engagement.'

'Congrats on the engagement. Do you need to book other guys or is this strictly about this cock?'

Torrie shivered. She loved when he talked straight and to the point.

'Me and you. Is that good?' she asked and waited.

'Perfect. It'll be good to see you again Torrie. I've thought about you. Keep it hot, moist and tight for me and I'll see you in a few weeks for MORE!'

Torrie deleted the text and placed her phone back in her purse.

"It's on and I'm ready. I'm ready for MORE," she said to herself.

She had the smile of a lottery winner on her face as she grabbed her documents for her meeting.

My Sister's Husband

1 – My Sister's Husband

"Ms. Nelson's office. Can I help you?"

"Trish, it's Tammi. Is my sister in today? I've been calling her cell phone because I thought she was off today and I haven't been getting an answer."

"Hi, Ms. Tammi. Yes, she's here. She was going to take the day off, but a big meeting came up and she didn't want to miss it."

"Oh, okay. Sounds like she's busy. I'll call he back later."

"No, no. She's finished with that and in her office. Hold on and I'll let her know you're on the line."

"Ms. Nelson, your sister is on the line."

Kandi lit up when she heard that her sister was on the phone. She grabbed her desk phone and pressed the button for the line that was lit up.

"Hey, sis. What's going on? I was going to call

you when I left. I'm going to the gym later on and wanted to see if you wanted to finally join me. You've been promising me that you would start going with me and I'm still waiting."

"Kandi, can I get a word in please and no I'm not going to the gym. I don't see myself turning into a workout fanatic like you."

"I'm not trying to turn you into a workout fanatic like me. I just want you to be healthy."

"I am healthy, just a few pounds overweight and besides, Jason loves my love handles. You'd have them too after pushing out a set of twins."

Kandi laughed and thought of her niece and nephew. They were everything to her since Tammi was her only sibling. Since she didn't have any children of her own, she loved the time she spent with the two, three-year olds. Tammi also had something else she didn't have; a husband. Though she'd like to have kids one day, she wasn't too sure of the husband part. She liked being single and loved her space. Maybe one day. For now, she'd continue with her serial dating habit and sampling as much good cock as she could in Maine.

"Whatever. So now that you can get in a word, what's going on? How are the kids?"

"They're good and definitely a handful. They are why I was calling you. Jason is out of town and isn't coming back until Sunday. I was hoping you could come over and keep the kids this weekend, just until Jason gets home Sunday morning."

"Where are you going that you'll be gone all weekend?"

"Remember I told you I was going to New York for the weekend to celebrate with Sherry for her thirtieth birthday. We've been friends since college and I don't want to miss this weekend. I never get to go anywhere with two three-year olds at home and I was looking forward to it. Jason was suppose to be home this weekend and got called away on business and now it looks like he won't fly back home until Sunday morning. That means I either have to miss the weekend or ask the babysitter and I'm not sure she's equipped to handle them for the entire weekend. With you, I never have to worry about them because they'll be in good hands. You take such good care of us."

"Alright Tammi. You don't have to butter me up. I didn't have any plans for this weekend other than to get laid, but I guess I can suppress that desire until I get back home."

"Ah, who is it this time? Someone old or someone new?"

"Someone new. I met him at a conference last week and I was thinking of having him over for some fun this weekend. After the conference we went dancing and when we danced, he rubbed what felt like a giant cock against me and all I could think about was who much I wanted to swallow him whole. We've talked a few times this week and last night the conversation got quite hot and heavy.

Only for my sister will I turn down the chance for a good fuck," she said laughing.

"Girl, you and that mouth of yours. I love that I have to live vicariously through you. Jason would think I was crazy if he heard me talk like that."

"You mean you and Jason don't talk nasty and dirty to each other to keep things alive?"

"Alive? You mean sex? I'm trying to remember what that is!" Tammi quipped.

"Wait, you've been married five years and already the sex is dying? That's why I'm staying single. I'd want sex with my husband to get hotter and hotter with each year, not lesser and lesser."

"Well, you don't have twins, a husband who travels and a non-profit agency to run. I know we need to do better and I know Jason wants more, but right now, life is so busy, there are nights we both crash in bed with our clothes still on. One day we'll get that magic back, but for now, I want to get to New York for some fun with the girls."

"Alright. You talked me into it. What time do you need me on Friday?"

"I'll pick the kids up from daycare at four. Anytime after that. I'll leave out whenever you get here."

"I'm taking off half-day on Friday, so why don't I pick them up and you go ahead and leave after you drop them off. I don't want you driving at night."

"Are you sure?" Tammi asked.

"Yes I'm sure. You know I love those kiddies and

since you're in a bind, I guess my personal life can wait a few days."

"You are the best. Thanks for always being there for me, the kids and Jason. We love you."

"I love you guys too. Since you're not going to the gym with me, I need to get off of here and get going. I had ice cream last night and I need to work it off."

"Seriously Kandi? You have no fat on that gorgeous body of yours. You have big, natural boobs, an ass that makes people confuse you with JLo when you walk and your beauty is why every modeling agency wanted to offer you a contract before you decided to go to college and get into politics instead. You live in the gym and still you need to be there more."

"More is my middle name and this body doesn't stay like this without some work. Since I can't get my usual workout in the sack this weekend, I guess the gym will have to do. Maybe I can get him to stop over tonight and hit me off before I head to your house tomorrow. I need to get it in wherever I can."

"I think I have a sex fiend for a sister," Tammi said.

"You only think? Oh yes, you definitely have a sister who's a sex fiend and if you don't turn into one, you and Jason are going to start having problems and I love you too much to see anything happen to your marriage. You need to do better."

"I know and I will. Can I tell you something

personal?"

"You know you can tell me anything," Kandi said.

"Okay, I know that I need to do better, but after I had the kids, my sex drive is not what it was before, but Jason's has increased. He wants it all the time and I just don't feel like it."

"So you just leave him with blue balls?" Kandi asked.

"No, Kandi. I usually give him blow jobs, but even I know that won't be enough for much longer. Taking care of the house, Jason, the kids and my position as the director at the non-profit, I'm exhausted and I can't keep up with his sex drive anymore. Maybe getting in the gym with you will help with my stamina. Let's plan on it starting next week."

"Sis, of course it will. That and you need to get nasty like a porn star and really put it on him. Learn some new tricks and flips and tire his ass out."

"Words of a sex fiend who's on her way to being a nymphomaniac. I know how you get down and not every woman loves sex as much as you do."

"There is nothing wrong with loving sex especially when it's fulfilling. I know you and Jason had a lot of good sex in the past and you just need to get back to that. You know we talk about everything and I remember your down and dirty stories. It's time to get back to that. Listen, I don't want to preach to you. Go have your fun in New York for the weekend and get a break from the kids, the house and everything else and focus only on having fun. I'll take care of everything at home. How's that?"

"Okay, that sounds perfect and I do need this weekend away. Thank you."

"I'll see you when you get back Sunday evening."

"Have fun with the kids. I won't tell them you're picking them up and staying with them for the weekend. They'll be extra excited since you spoil them crazy."

"They love me," Kandi said.

"You spoil them," Tammi said.

"Aunts were created to spoil nieces and nephews and I take that job very serious. I'll talk to you Friday. I'm leaving work to see if I can squeeze in a marathon sex session to last me through the weekend. You will owe me big time for this."

"I got you!" Tammi exclaimed before hanging up.

2 – My Sister's Husband

"Jason Houser, is that you?"

Jason turned around when he heard his name being called. He had just gotten off of his plane and was exhausted, too exhausted to get pulled into a lengthy conversation. As soon as he saw Jimmy, he knew the conversation would get dragged out.

"Jimmy! How are you buddy," he said.

"I'm good. You coming or going?"

"Just getting home. I was going to fly in on Sunday, but the guy I replaced at a conference ended up coming after all, so I didn't need to stay the whole time. I figured I'd fly home early and surprise the family, though the kids are probably asleep by now."

"I'm on my way out, heading to Colorado to visit a new resort my brother is opening. How's business?"

Jason was hoping he could get away after a few

lines of chit chat, but that didn't seem like it was going to happen.

"Business is great. I'm running the east coast division now, so they're working me hard, but it's all paid off. How are things with you business-wise?"

"I can't complain. I'm thinking of transferring to another office in a few months. I'm trying to get away from this cold, Maine weather and get to a warmer climate."

"Good for you. I grew up in a warm climate and now I love the cold Maine winters. Well, have a safe trip and maybe we can get the families together for dinner or something soon," Jason said.

"How are Tammi and the kids doing? The twins are three years old now right?"

"Yes and they're getting bigger every day. Tammi does a great job considering they are a handful and I spend a lot of time at the office."

"Sounds like the two of you could use a weekend away at my brother's resort. I'll bring back some information."

"Sounds good. I'll see you soon Jimmy and it was good running into you."

Jason turned and walked away before Jimmy could ask any more questions. He was anxious to get home to Tammi. He felt bad that she had to miss her weekend in New York with her friends because he had to fly out of town on business. He was still getting in later than he'd planned, but this way, they could spend some time together since the kids would be asleep.

As he walked to his car, he thought about the state of their marriage and knew that they needed to find a way to get the sex back into the marriage. He was spending too many nights jacking off or going to bed after taking an ice cold shower. He loved his wife and was trying to be patient, but his libido was taking a serious hit. He walked around in a constant state of arousal. It wasn't that they never had sex, but it wasn't as frequent or as wild as it had been in the past. At thirty-two years old, he shouldn't have to resort to jacking off or begging his wife to do more than blow him. He loved a blow-job as much as the next guy, but sliding in between some nice soft legs was still top on his list.

Getting in his car which he'd left at the airport and finally making his way through traffic, he noticed the time on the car console read midnight. He hoped Tammi was still awake and that he could persuade her into some hot sex after apologizing profusely for being the cause of her missing the party.

Tammi had been upset when he called to tell her that he'd be delayed until Sunday. He tried calling her twice since they argued and she wouldn't answer her cell phone or the house phone. Giving her a break, he decided to wait until he got home to make up with her. He was hoping by making up, it meant fucking her brains out like a starving man.

Driving, images of him sliding his nine-inch cock into her sweet, moist pussy had him moving around in his seat to adjust his growing penis. Tammi could to take him deep and ride him like he was a stallion horse. He loved dipping his head between her legs and didn't even mind the times she'd closed her thighs on his head as her orgasm slammed into her. When she rode his tongue, he loved lapping her essence as it flowed out of her and into his mouth. Those were the days, he thought as he used one hand to massage his hard cock. They were overdue for a night like that.

Taking the shortest route home, Jason pulled up to his house and decided against parking in the garage. The kids' rooms were above the garage and he didn't want anything to wake them. Nothing was going to keep him from laying pipe to his wife tonight. He parked in front of the house, grabbed his bag from the trunk and quietly walked in the darkened house. Apparently Tammi had gone to bed, though he knew her to stay up late most Friday nights after putting the kids to bed.

Not bothering to turn on any lights, he crept up the steps and stopped first at each of the kid's rooms. Seeing them sound asleep, he pulled their doors closed all the way, though Tammy like for them to be open in case one of them woke up in the middle of the night. He would double back after his planned seduction and reopen their doors.

Walking the short distance to his bedroom, even

in the darkness, he could see the frame of Tammi's body under the cover. She was asleep on her side with her ass pointed right at him. Her body was completely covered by the comforter and he couldn't wait to slide underneath it behind her, letting his cock poke her in the ass. If she didn't wake up from that, the minute he entered her, he felt sure she'd wake up then. He remember a time when she loved when he did that. First he would get a shower and then come back to cater to her. She had to have the same need that he did. There was a time when she liked fucking all the time.

Rather than wake her by the running of the shower, he dropped his bag on the floor and went to take a shower in the downstairs bathroom. Before turning around to head back downstairs, he stood watching Tammi as she slept and imagined all of the nasty, naughty and dirty things he wanted to do to her.

He wanted to eat her pussy and tongue fuck her until she came in his mouth. Then he wanted to slide up into her and pound like a dying man while nipping and sucking her tits. They weren't as big as he would like, but they were hers and he loved them.

Now Kandi, her sister had a rack of tits for days. He has imagined, more than a few times, what her tits would look and feel like. He knew that Kandi had a very active sex life. He'd heard a few of Tammi's conversations with her and he also knew a guy or two who had fucked her and told him how unbelievably good she was in bed. Fantasizing about Kandi was doing no harm and a few times in the shower, he imagined the sight of her with her mouth wide open taking his entire cock in her mouth. Word was she was a blow-job queen.

Tammi was good at giving him head, though he'd like it a little more sloppy and porn-like.

Now that he was rock hard, it was time for a shower so that he could get back to bed. Removing clothes as he walked to the lower level bathroom, Jason turned on the shower and hopped in. Closing his eyes, he temporarily thought again about Kandi. Why she was on his mind all of a sudden he didn't know. It could be the conversation one of his buddies had with him a week ago when apparently he and Kandi had fucked after they ran into each other at the store.

He liked that Kandi was free sexually and had no misgivings about giving up her sweet pussy. He's even heard a story or two about her being with a guy and another woman at the same time. Now that was his fantasy, but he knew Tammi would never go for that.

He imagined Kandi's big ass tits swinging back and forth while he took her doggy style, one of his favorite positions. He'd heard how wild she was and wild got him off.

As the water cascaded down, Jason felt his cock rise and get hard and guiltily it wasn't with thoughts of his wife, but with thoughts of her hot sister. Tammi was still as sexy as ever, but knowing how naughty Kandi was and adding to that how sexy she was, she turned him on. He briefly thought about jacking himself off while thinking about Kandi on all fours, but instead, stopped, finished his shower and got out. He needed to be in some pussy.

Turning off the shower and grabbing a towel, he toweled off before wrapping the towel around his hips and walking back to the bedroom. The tent the towel made was how hard his cock was and nothing was going to satisfy him besides fucking. He needed to wake his wife.

Jason walked into the bedroom and closed the door all the way, removing all light from the room thanks to the window blinds that blocked out all light. He dropped the towel and slowly climbed into bed behind Tammi. Reaching under the comforter, he rubbed her ass softly and was surprised to see that she was wearing a thong. Tammi hated thongs, but his cock hardened even more at the thought of her nice ass in a thong. He'd buy them for her and she'd hide them in the back of the dresser, instead preferring to wear sexy, lacy bikini panties, which he also loved.

Sliding his hand over her ass, he moved down to caress her leg as he moved closer so that his cock was pressing up against her ass. He looked and still she hadn't woke up. In the darkness, he had to go by her movements since he couldn't see her clearly and the comforter still covered her with the exception of her ass.

Rubbing his cock across her ass, Jason reached between her legs and lightly stroked her pussy lips through her thong. She must have recently shaved or waxed because he didn't encounter any trace of hair, something he often did. She never shaved her pussy hair all the way off, preferring instead to leave a little, thin layer of hair. He loved the smooth feeling of her pussy lips without hair on them. Leaning down he placed a soft kiss on one of the globes of her ass while he slipped a finger between her legs even further until he encountered the entrance to her pussy. Lightly finger fucking her, he felt a little movement of her hips. He smiled knowing Tammi was slowly coming awake as he had planned for her to do. Increasing the pressure of his finger and using his thumb to stroke her clit, his cock twitched when he heard a soft mewl escape her lips. Now she was ready, he thought.

"Wake up, baby. I'm horny and I need to get in this pussy," he said, going back to using nasty words she loved in the past and they'd somehow gotten away from. He ground his hips even more into her ass cheek.

"I have a big, fat hard-on that's ready to slide right into you. Are you ready for me baby? Are you waking up?"

He felt her moving even more and heard her

moans get louder.

"Tammi?" he said reaching to turn her over. As he did, she suddenly sat up and leaped out of the bed screaming, practically terrorizing him.

"What the fuck are you doing?" he heard and familiarity set in and it wasn't a sound or words he'd ever heard Tammi say. In fact, she didn't sound like Tammi at all. He must be dreaming because it actually sounded like Kandi. Suddenly the lights came on and as his eyes adjusted to the brightened room, he opened his eyes and they landed on Kandi and not Tammi. Realizing what had just happened, he leaned back out of fear and fell to the floor.

"Jason, what the fuck?"

3 – My Sister's Husband

"Oh my goodness," Jason said.

Kandi tried her best to cover herself to no avail. Jason could see that she was wearing a tiny t-shirt that barely covered her large breasts.

"Jason!"

"Kandi, look, I'm sorry. I thought you were Tammi and what are you doing in my bed? Where is Tammi?" he asked.

"She's in New York at a girl's weekend. She asked me to come over this weekend and watch the kids because you weren't due back until Sunday. What are you doing back already?"

Jason noticed that they were chatting as if she wasn't standing in front of him almost naked. He was still naked and now standing trying to put the towel he'd dropped to the floor over his hardness. He was ashamed to say, seeing Kandi in no bra and a t-shirt and thong was making him even harder.

"I took an early flight back, feeling bad that she was going to have to miss her getaway because of me. I'm sorry. I didn't know it was you in bed, I thought it was Tammi."

"Didn't you see my car in the garage?" Kandi said while trying to keep her eyes from his hard cock.

"I didn't park in the garage. When we come in late, we park on the street so the opening and closing of the garage door doesn't wake the kids."

Jason stood to get the towel fully around his waist, trying hard to cover his rising cock. Damn, he thought. Even in this situation, his cock wouldn't go down. He looked over at Kandi and saw her smile and then she broke out in a fit of laughter.

"What the hell is so funny? Do you know what almost happened?" Jason said.

"What? You were about to fuck your wife from behind until you discovered it was me? You did finger me you know and that's what woke me up."

Jason looked at her shocked at the words that came out her mouth.

"Seriously Kandi? You got jokes at a time like this? I need to find some clothes."

Jason looked around for anything he could find to slip on.

"Don't on my account. From where I'm standing, you may injure yourself if you try to stuff that thing inside of some pants still hard like that."

Jason looked down at his cock and it was

standing at full attention.

"Okay, now you're teasing and you need to stop."

Kandi walked back to the bed and got back in, laying down and facing his side of the room, resting her head in her hand, looking as if she wasn't going anywhere.

"Stop what? You're the one standing here with a raging hard-on and from the looks of things, you're packing quite a bit under that towel."

Jason shook his head to be sure he wasn't dreaming. Was his hot sister-in-law flirting with him? He turned in the direction of the closet and grabbed his robe, dropped the towel and put the robe on. Now the tent was in his robe just as it had been in his towel. He needed to concentrate on something to make it go down. Seeing and thinking about Kandi in his bed wasn't going to do the trick.

"Well, now that I'm home, you can go home."

Kandi sucked her teeth.

"I'm not leaving, at least not at this minute. I'm having too much fun watching you squirm."

"Not funny Kandi."

"It's hilarious."

"Do you know where I had my finger? This is not funny at all. Tammi would kill me," he exclaimed with a serious tone.

"We won't tell her and you'll live to feel me up another day and yes I know where your finger was and it felt good."

Seconds passed by with them staring at each

other. He didn't know what to say next since the moment was the most awkward of his life.

"We should not be having this conversation. I'll go sleep on the sofa and you can have the bed."

"Why?"

"Why what?"

"Why are you going to sleep on the sofa?" she asked.

"Are you going to sleep on the sofa?"

"Hell no," Kandi said, shifting around on the bed.

Jason's eyes drifted to her tits which showed through the thin layer of her t-shirt. He could see her big, round nipples and the tips had begun to pebble. He was in trouble. He cleared his throat and redirected his eyes.

"Well, one of us has to since that's the only other sleeping area in the house. Look, I'm sorry for touching you like that. I swear I thought it was Tammi," he said nervously.

Kandi smiled hoping to calm his nervousness.

"Jason, it's okay. I'd say Tammi was a very lucky woman."

He watched as Kandi's eyes darted down to his cock which still had not gone down. He had a feeling as long as she laid across his bed like she was waiting for him, it wouldn't. He needed to get out of the room before he further embarrassed himself.

"I would say thanks, but I'm not sure I should."

"Jason, chill the fuck out. Don't get all crazy over this. It was an honest mistake. Now, it could be considered a problem if you felt me up now, since you know it's me and not Tammi. I understand you two are having a few problems in the bedroom and I can't for the life of me understand why. What you're packing, I'd be on it every day."

His cock was officially harder than it's ever been in his entire life. The image of her riding him flooded his head and wouldn't go away. He knew he should turn and walk out of the room, but he was too intrigued.

"Tammi talks to you about our sex life?"

"Well, actually she talks to me about the lack of it. She explained to me that she hasn't felt much like fucking these days, leaving you with blue balls I hear. That's not a good thing. Like right now, I can tell how hard you are and that must be painful," she purred.

Jason didn't know what to say and swallowed hard, holding back the words he wanted to say, which would make the scene even weirder. He wanted to tell her that his cock would go down only if he could bury it deep inside of her, but that would be wrong on every level possible.

"What are you doing, Kandi? We should stop this banter."

Kandi wasn't planning to stop anything. When she woke to the feeling of a finger going in and out of her pussy, she realized she wasn't dreaming.

When she discovered what was happening, she was frightened at first and now, she was horny and wanted to fuck. Tammi would never know.

The night before, she was unable to reach the friend she was going to hang out with over the weekend, hoping to catch him for a quick fuck. Instead, she was horny and had her eyes glued to a big ass cock, even though it belonged to her sister's husband. Right now, she didn't care who it belonged to, she wanted it.

Kandi slid closer to his side of the bed, feeling her t-shirt slide further up her body, exposing even more of her body to his view.

"Don't try and act like you haven't thought about what it would be like to fuck me. Stan told me he shared with you that we ran into each other in the store recently and went back to my house and fucked for over an hour before he had to get home to his wife. Women will never learn to not talk about their husband's sexual prowess. They give another woman insight into what it would be like with them and I have no problem finding out for myself at that point. He was good, but I bet you'd be better. I can tell your cock is bigger."

Jason was stunned that he was standing in his bedroom listening to his sister-in-law say fuck as if they often had conversations like this. If she was going to play the game, he was going to play along with her.

"Yeah, well, thinking about it and doing it are

two very different things. One could land me in divorce court and losing my kids and nothing is worth that."

Kandi moved, exposing even more of her body.

"Are you sure about that? What have you heard about me? Come on, no one is in this room, but you and me and I promise I would never tell Tammi we're talking like this and we're just talking."

"You should fix your shirt," he said between clinched teeth. Jason found that he was having a hard time concentrating with her big, gorgeous tits beckoning him.

"Why, you've never seen tits before?"

"I've never seen yours before and I'm sure I shouldn't be seeing them now."

"Shh," she said, putting her finger to her lips to quiet him.

"We need to stop this," Jason said, knowing he was getting more turned on by the minute.

"Don't talk so loud. Why don't you come closer so that we don't have to talk loud."

Jason didn't move because he was afraid to and his idea to will his cock to go down was having the opposite effect.

"Kandi, stop it," he whispered.

"What did you say? I can't hear you unless you come closer."

She slid even further across the bed until she was now laying across it diagonally with her ass in the air and her tits hanging out even further.

"This is dangerous ground we're treading on."

"You can leave this room anytime you want. I'm not stopping you, but I wish you would come closer. Come here," she said seductively.

Jason felt like a moth to a frame and when he watched Kandi stick her tongue out and lick her lips, he could no longer resist. All he could think about was her mouth on his cock. With that in mind, he moved closer to the bed.

"I know you can hear me now," he said nervously.

"I don't know Jason. I'm thinking just a little bit closer," she said summoning him with her finger.

Kandi knew that one more step and she'd be inches away from his cock being within her reach, which is where she wanted him. Blame it on her sister for telling her how good Jason's cock was. Shame on her for not giving up the pussy on a consistent basis and leaving her man with a hard cock or a cold shower.

"Damn, you are fine," he said before it was too late to take it back.

"Yes, I am and I know how to keep a secret. What about you? Do you know how to keep a secret Jason?"

"I do if my life depends on it," he admitted.

Kandi reached out and tugged him by his robe until the cloth rubbed against her face.

"I'd say your life depends on you learning to keep a secret tonight. What do you think?" she said looking up at him.

"I'd say I agree with you."

"You know, I gave up something to watch the kids this weekend. Want to know what that was?" she said seductively watching him as he eyed her tits even longer.

Jason cleared his throat again. He wanted her so bad, knowing he shouldn't, but he couldn't help himself. She was the tigress he needed, especially now that his cock was rock-solid hard and nothing was making it go down.

"What was that?" he whispered.

Kandi reached out and rubbed the softness of the soft velour blue robe he wore, not touching the area tented by his big cock.

"I'm horny and I was supposed to be getting fucked about right now actually. I had a friend who I met recently and I wanted to feel him sliding into me and taking the edge of a busy week off. I haven't had that done yet and I'm still feeling the edge. What do you say about that?"

Jason tried to respond and when he opened his mouth to do so, the words got caught in his throat the moment he felt Kandi rub the tip of her finger over the ridge of his cock through the robe.

"I...I...don't know what to say about that," he stuttered out.

Kandi didn't look up at him, but focused on his cock pressing against the inside of his robe. Reaching inside of his robe, she took hold of his hardness and stroked up and down as she heard his breaths get deeper and ragged.

"Would you like to fuck me, Jason?" she asked.

Not giving him a chance to answer, she looked up into his face, opened her mouth while she pulled his cock through the slit in the robe and licked the head of his cock. She licked across the slit in the head before running her tongue around the large head.

"Ohhh," Jason crooned, while involuntarily moving his hips toward her mouth.

"Should I take it your answer is yes?" she said and then opening wider, she took as much of his cock into her mouth as she could get. Not holding back, she sucked him as she felt his legs quiver. As her mouth worked him, she added hand motion and stroked his cock while she sucked him.

Jason groaned, not believing he was looking down at Kandi with his cock in her mouth. Any thoughts of not fucking her went out the window as he untied the robe and dropped it to the floor.

"Damn, your mouth is good. Suck it harder for me."

Kandi loved the feel of his cock in her mouth so much that she didn't need to be asked to suck him harder. She went to town slobbering all over his cock until she had enough wetness that he felt velvety going in and out of her mouth. This is what she craved all the time.

"That's it. I've dreamed about this," Jason said,

holding on to her head to guide her just like he dreamed of, only now this was reality and everything he'd heard about her blow-job skills was better than the stories. He had to curl his toes to keep from shoving his cock further in her mouth. He felt the tension rising and knew that if he was going to do this and have it be the only time, he wanted more. Stepping back until his cock popped out of her mouth, he turned her over and spun her around on the bed until he could pull her by her legs until her ass rested on the edge of the mattress.

"Hungry?" she asked, smiling up at him as she removed the t-shirt from her body releasing her big tits.

Jason's eyes nearly popped out of his head. Her tits were more beautiful than he even imagined.

"You are so fucking hot."

"Yes, I am. Eat me," she said.

Needing no instructions, Jason went down on his knees in between her widespread legs and pushed them back toward her head opening her completely to him. Not wasting time with removing her thong, he slid it to the side and dove in with his mouth. The first pass of his tongue garnered a sexy moan from Kandi as she ground her hips into his face.

"That's it, Jason. Your tongue feels so good," she moaned and crooned.

"You taste delicious," Jason said and dived in again, this time focusing on her clit and rubbing his entire face in her pussy. It wasn't long before he felt her body shake as she stifled the scream that was about to exit her mouth as she came into his.

Kandi was losing control. Her body was flying so high, she wasn't sure she'd be able to come down. Jason was eating her like she'd never been eaten out before and quicker than she'd ever come before, she exploded on his tongue as a bright light flashed across her eyelids. Her orgasm went on and one. Not giving her time to rest, excitement went through her as Jason stood and positioned his cock at the entrance to her pussy.

"I've been dying to fuck you."

"Do it," she urged. "Fuck me, Jason. I want your big cock in me."

"I've dreamed about fucking you. Are you ready?" he asked, just before he surged forward going inside of her until he was completed seated inside of her.

"Oh, yes!" she said as he lifted her legs over his shoulders and pounded deep and hard adding a grind to his hips increasing the erotic feel of his cock fucking her tight pussy.

"Give it to me hard!" Kandi said, forceful, but quietly.

Jason planted his feet solidly and gave in to his desire to fuck her relentlessly. Seeing how much she was enjoying it was all he needed. The wet, sloppy sounds of his cock going in and out of her had him staying harder than he thought was possible. Kandi was wild and nasty just like he liked and like he heard she was. She was pushing into him with every stroke he surged into her.

"I'm coming," she uttered before her body crashed over and over as her orgasm slammed into her causing her to ride his cock even harder.

"Yes, yes, yes!" Jason said, trying not to scream. After several more pumps, he felt his orgasm about to rip free, so he pulled out of her body as he stroked himself with his hand until he squirted all over her stomach as he tried to focus through blurry vision.

"Wow," Kandi said when Jason attempted to catch his breath.

"I'm not done yet," he said when he opened his eyes.

Kandi looked down at his cock and noticed he was still hard. Before she could say anything, Jason had turned her over until she was on her knees and without words, he pushed into her from behind. He leaned forward and groped her large tits while he fucked her from behind.

"I can't tell you how much I've wanted to fuck you like this," he said into her ear as he licked and sucked on the lobe.

Kandi had been with quite a few men, but being with Jason was the best she'd had in a long time and to know that he kept a hard-on even after an earth shattering orgasm enticed her even more. The thought had her body humming again as she surged back against his powerful strokes.

"That's it, fuck me baby," he moaned in her ear.

Hearing him and feeling him, Kandi did just that. She loved it hard and deep and that's just how Jason was giving it to her. She had already experienced two powerful orgasms and already she felt a third start at her toes and quickly flow through her body. Before long, she felt her body gush at the same time that Jason groaned into her ear while gushing inside of her body as his orgasm flowed through him causing them both to collapsed onto the bed, breathing as if they'd just run a marathon.

Kandi couldn't speak. She had never been pleasured so thoroughly and to think the best fucking she'd ever had, came from her brother-in-law. As her body calmed, she realized the good fucking she'd had planned for the weekend, she'd actually gotten.

4 – My Sister's Husband

"Hey, sis! I'm home after a much needed weekend away. Jason told me he came home early. Thanks for looking after the kids until he came home. I hope it wasn't too much of an imposition since I know you had plans originally."

"Hey Tammi. Don't worry about it. When did you get in?" Kandi asked.

"About an hour ago and I had a good time. It was so much fun, though I missed the kids like crazy. They told me you made them pizza and chicken nuggets, their favorite. You are the best aunt any kid can have."

"Hey, I do what I can do, when I can do it. I'm glad you had fun. You need to find more time to get a break when you need it and I'll always be around to step in to your role when you need to get away."

Kandi felt ashamed that she was speaking more

of stepping into her sister's role as far as her wifely duties are concerned, though she would also watch the kids whenever he was needed.

"You know, I was telling Jason that very thing and he made the same suggestion you did. Oh, I forgot to tell you that you left one of your bags here that had some clothes in it."

"Oh, I'll get that from you soon."

"Don't worry about it. Jason said he had to go out for a bit and he offered to drop it off at your house. He should be arriving soon."

As soon as Tammi spoke the words, her door bell rang and on the other side of the door was Jason.

"If you're not there when he gets there, I told him to use my spare key and leave it in your house. I hope that's okay."

"I'll be here when he gets here," she said signaling for him not to speak as she pointed to the phone and mouthed Tammi's name. Jason, understanding entered quietly.

"Thanks again for taking care of my family while I was gone."

"Hey, that's what sisters are for. I will always take care of your family," she said.

"I'll call you later. When Jason gets there, tell him to stop on his way back later and bring something for dinner."

"I sure will. I'll give him the message."

After she hung up the phone, Kandi turned around to see Jason standing before her with his cock in his hand, stroking it to a powerful, thick, fat length.

"You are supposed to take care of her family right? I hope that still extends to me," Jason said.

"Oh, it extends especially to you," Kandi said, stepping closer to him and going down on her knees and licking her lips as Jason slid his cock between her lips.

"Yes!" Jason uttered. He looked forward to he and Kandi continuing to take care of each other.

Enjoy my first two erotic novels, Cheating Swingers: Naughty Sex Chronicles, Volume 1 by C. Nookie and Strange Desires: Naughty Sex Chronicles, Volume 2 by C. Nookie available for download and in paperback.

Stay tuned for, Part 2 of Cheating Swingers: Naughty Sex Chronicles, Volume 3, coming in November 2016.

The saga continues....